F★CKFACE

F★CKFACE

And Other Stories

Leah Hampton

HENRY HOLT AND COMPANY

NEW YORK

Henry Holt and Company
Publishers since 1866
120 Broadway
New York, New York 10271
www.henryholt.com

Henry Holt® and ® are registered trademarks of Macmillan Publishing Group, LLC.

Some of these stories have appeared elsewhere, in slightly different form: "Meat" in *Electric Literature*'s Recommended Reading, August 21, 2019; "Parkway" in *Ecotone*, Winter 2018; "Boomer" in *North Carolina Literary Review*, vol. 26 (2018) online; "Sparkle" in *Appalachian Heritage*, Winter 2017; "Fuckface" in *storySouth*, Spring 2016; "Queen" in *Appalachian Heritage*, Summer 2014; "The Saint" in *North Carolina Literary Review*, vol. 22 (2013).

Library of Congress Cataloging-in-Publication Data

Names: Hampton, Leah, author.
Title: F*ckface : and other stories / by Leah Hampton.
Description: First edition. | New York : Henry Holt and Company, 2020. |
Identifiers: LCCN 2019040534 (print) | LCCN 2019040535 (ebook) |
    ISBN 9781250259592 (hardcover) | ISBN 9781250259585 (ebook)
Classification: LCC PS3608.A695963 A6 2020 (print) | LCC PS3608.A695963
    (ebook) | DDC 813/.6—dc23
LC record available at https://lccn.loc.gov/2019040534
LC ebook record available at https://lccn.loc.gov/2019040535

Our books may be purchased in bulk for promotional, educational, or business use. Please contact your local bookseller or the Macmillan Corporate and Premium Sales Department at (800) 221-7945, extension 5442, or by e-mail at MacmillanSpecialMarkets@macmillan.com.

First Edition 2020

Designed by Meryl Sussman Levavi

Printed in the United States of America

1 3 5 7 9 10 8 6 4 2

This is a work of fiction. All of the characters, organizations, and events portrayed in this collection either are products of the author's imagination or are used fictitiously.

For David, who helped me find them

"You cannot save the land apart from the people, or the people apart from the land."

—WENDELL BERRY

Contents

F★CKFACE

FUCKFACE

Nothing'll ever fix what's broken in this town, but it would be nice if they'd at least get the dead bear out of the parking lot at Food Country.

Me and my friend Jamie and everybody who worked at the store had been staring at that bear for a week. It wasn't full grown, but it was still fat from eating all summer, so the body was hard to miss. Carter asked around a few places and couldn't get an answer about what to do with it. He said even the park service wouldn't come collect it. Carter's only the assistant manager, but us checkers always fetch him when something needs doing. There's no point asking the real manager.

Jamie reckoned somebody ran over the bear in the night and brought it to the back of the store to throw it in the dumpster. She said they were probably thinking they could hide it, but our dumpsters have locks on them, so they wound up just leaving it there. Bear season wasn't for a few more weeks, so the bear killer, whoever it was, didn't want to get in trouble, she guessed.

Carter and me and Jamie sat out on the picnic table behind the store looking at it. We had to walk past the bear whenever we went back there for a smoke break or brought out trash. I said it seemed like surely somebody in authority would clean it up. Animal control maybe? One of the cops from Bryson City? Carter just shook his head.

"Infrastructure," he said.

Jamie nodded. I looked at both of them and dragged on my vape. "Huh?"

Carter put his hands on his stout thighs and nodded at the bear lump. The blood was black on it now. Its head was flopped at an angle, facing away from us, but I knew its eyes were open.

"Infrastructure," he said again. He sneered, and I could see where the wrinkles would be on his doughy face in twenty years or so. "As in, we don't have any. No tax base in Robbinsville, Enn-See. Nobody gives a shit about a bear on private property, unless it's at one of the rental places. But tourist season's over. So."

Carter tapped his feet and looked at the ridge of mountains hanging above us.

"So nobody's gonna help us take care of it?" I said.

Jamie put her chin on the picnic table and stared at the bear. "We could get Travis to move it," she said. "Travis is an asshole. He probably put it there in the first place."

Carter shook his head. "We're not supposed to touch it. Could have diseases. It's a legal thing. Corporate office told Fuckface he couldn't make us move it."

Fuckface was what we called the store manager, our real boss.

Fuckface never left his office for anything; he just kept to himself. Most of us didn't even know his real name. Ever since I started working at Food Country my junior year of high school, I'd only seen him out on the floor twice. Once was on my first day. Jamie was training me on register and told me he didn't even care that we called him Fuckface, as long as our drawers were straight at the end of our shift. I remember he walked by right when she said it, and all I could think was how sharp looking he was, with his clothes ironed crisp, and how round and scary his eyes were. He reminded me of the principal at my old middle school—the one who got fired a while back for giving condoms to some Christian kids.

"Why do y'all call him Fuckface?" I whispered. I figured maybe he'd screwed one of the checkout girls or something. Jamie shook her head slow. She watched him pass, then turned to me and smiled. "Who gives a shit?" she said, and we killed ourselves laughing. We were good friends after that, and Carter always scheduled our shifts together.

"Still," said Jamie, squinting at the bear. "I bet Travis would move it if you gave him ten dollars."

"I'd get in trouble," said Carter. He tapped his gold assistant manager's name tag. "Travis isn't supposed to lift over fifty pounds. It's a rule for stockers." He moved his hand up and rubbed the acne on his neck. "And y'all aren't supposed to be smoking those fake cigarettes. Even out here."

Jamie shivered and turned her head so her cheek rested on the picnic table. Her hair fell down across her back and hung below the top of the table. She had one hand between her knees, and the other held her vape and rested on the bench. Her fingers were so tiny and thin. I wished I could wear rings the way she did, but my fingers were too stubby. It was beautiful, Jamie sitting there like that. I watched her for a long time. I think maybe Carter did, too.

"Pretty, are you getting off at six?" asked Jamie. Her head was turned away from us.

"Yeah, why?" I said.

Jamie lifted her head. "Can I have a ride home?" Her eyeliner was smudged, and she looked even more tired than I felt. She looked like she was far away.

***

My register gets the most traffic because I'm on the end. People think I'm the express lane, but Food Country doesn't have express lanes. Nothing in this town does; the mountains stop everything from moving.

I try to be quick when somebody comes with a basket instead of a cart, but today I was moving slow. I hadn't slept the night before because the trailer next to ours was having some kind of bullshit barbecue until three. It's just me and my dad living there now; momma found herself a boyfriend last year and told me I was old enough to figure out my own life. Back in the day my dad would have kicked ass over all that noise, but he won't do anything to the neighbors anymore. He's worried if cops start sniffing around, the county might cut his disability checks.

I couldn't focus on my register at all. My feet hurt, and I kept checking the clock under my receipt display.

"Pretty," said this big redheaded woman at me. She had a basket full of tampons and dill-pickle-flavored potato chips.

"Yeah," I said.

"That's your name? Pretty?" the redheaded woman said. She was staring at my name tag, not smiling. I'd never seen her in the store before.

"Yeah," I said.

She watched me close. I could feel her watching while I dragged her tampons across the scanner a third time. They didn't beep.

"How come your momma and daddy called you that?"

I shrugged and called Travis on the PA to price check the tampons.

"Well," the redhead said. "You need to live up to your name better, young lady. Got your hair all cut off."

Behind me, I heard Jamie slap her drawer shut hard.

"You oughta grow that hair out." She leaned over and frowned at my sneakers. "Get you some decent shoes, too."

The tampons finally beeped, so I canceled the price check. I finished ringing up the woman, bagged her chips. As she walked out, Jamie hissed at her. I looked over at Jamie and she smiled. I wished I could tell her how beautiful she was, but I figured she already knew.

Carter came by a few minutes later and told me to clear my drawer if I wanted. It was almost six. Then his shoulders slumped, and he said, "And try not to send Travis on price checks in Feminine Hygiene. Or if you do, don't cancel them after he goes down that aisle. He's pissed. Thinks you did it on purpose."

"Jesus, Carter, he's just . . . whatever."

"I know. Get on home now."

I waved at Jamie and told her I'd meet her at my car.

***

We were both hungry, so we went to the Wing King before I took her home. I can't drink yet, but Jamie turned twenty-one last winter. I was parking the hatchback when Jamie yawned and said, "I hate this fucking town. I'm moving to Asheville."

"It sucks here," I agreed. "You think Wing King's got a bear in their back lot?"

"I'm serious this time, Pretty," she said. She patted my dashboard and wiggled in her seat, then she tilted her head toward me. "Andrew got the job."

Jamie's boyfriend had been trying to get hired at a brewery in Asheville for months. "For real?" I said. My guts went tight.

She laughed, and the light bounced off the rings and stones stuck in her ear. "Yeah. I've been dying to tell you. He got it." She looked out my windshield. "I'm so done with this place."

We went into the Wing King and ordered food, and Jamie got a pitcher. She said she'd share with me if I reminded her to get some dessert to take home to her papaw. Her papaw was going to give her and Andrew the deposit on an apartment.

"Asheville is expensive," she said, shaking her head.

We sat for a while not saying much. I stared at Jamie, her long hair with all its wispy highlights, not believing she would really do it, really go. It wasn't like I was in love with her, but maybe I was. She was different, smarter than everybody else here, and she didn't care that I liked girls. I never even had to tell her; she just figured it out and didn't give me a hard time about it. Nobody else knows. Not that anybody would ever ask me what I like or don't like. But if they found out, I'd be in trouble all over. This place is a long way from Asheville—eighty miles, and a lot of churches in between.

"So, what do you think?" she asked after she'd finished half the pitcher.

I shrugged.

"Pretty," she said, "come on! Aren't you excited?" It was easy for Jamie; everything was easy for her. She went to Asheville all the time. For me, it might as well have been the moon.

I tried to swallow the burger chunk I was chewing, but it got stuck. I felt like I had to say something, so I took a big swig of beer and mumbled, "I bet you get a job at the Orange Peel or somewhere. That'd be cool."

Jamie rattled her shoulders, twitched her nose. "I hate that place," she said. "Those people who go there are so . . ." She looked around the bar for the word. "Entitled," she said finally.

"What do you mean?" I said. I knew what "entitled" meant, but I didn't want to talk.

"They're just full of shit. Think they're the center of the universe. Like you know we went to the concert last night?"

"Yeah," I said. "I'd been wanting to ask. I figured you'd come in to work talking all about it today. What'd she sing?"

One time, Jamie played me a CD of this woman, Joan Armatrading. She's old, and her songs are sad and weird, but I liked her. Jamie said those songs made her whole body float, and she listened to them all the time. When her boyfriend surprised her with tickets to the concert, she screamed and jumped on him right in front of the customers. She had skipped work last night to go to that show; that was why she was so tired all day. I realized now her boyfriend must have found out he got the job and bought the tickets off a scalper to celebrate. He said the show sold out months ago. Maybe that was part of why I hadn't slept the night before. Maybe I'd been thinking about the concert, and Jamie in the front row, listening to those weird songs, swaying her hair around, floating.

"It was good. I cried, it was so good," she said. "Except this one lady in the audience got really drunk and kept standing up and talking to Joan Armatrading like she was the only person in the room. She kept slurring and shouting about how beautiful Joan was, and everyone fucking hated it and couldn't hear the music, but no one said anything."

"Why not?" I figured Jamie would have raised a stink.

"Because it's Hippietown. And"—she pursed her lips tight—"I mean, she was missing a hand."

"Missing a *hand*?"

"Yeah, she was some kind of amputee. Her right hand was just—" She made a fist with her right hand, glided her left palm over it. My eyes got big. She took a gulp of beer.

"So no one wanted to yell at her," she went on. "Also, I think people were creeped out by her clapping." She picked up a wing bone off her plate and sucked on it.

"How could she even clap?"

Jamie put her chicken bone down and held up her fist again. "She kept slapping her left hand against her . . . you know. Nub."

Outside, a scrawny kid cycled by on a beat-up Schwinn. I watched him through the window and pulled a grim face; little kids shouldn't be alone on this end of town after dark.

"It was embarrassing. Stupid," she said. "That one-handed old cunt basically ruined the show."

"That sucks," I said. It was hard to think of what to say, except anything that made noise and kept her from talking about leaving.

"Yeah," said Jamie. "I was pissed. I was so excited for that concert.

That was the first time I'd ever seen her. Probably be the last, too. She doesn't tour much. I saw that one-handed woman afterwards in the street. I almost kicked her ass."

"Sounds like she had it coming," I said. "You should have."

She shrugged again. "Nobody wants to be the bitch who sucker punches a gimp at the Joan Armatrading show."

"Sure," I replied, nodding. "Sure thing."

"Anyway," said Jamie. "I don't want to work there. The Orange Peel. I'll get a job at the mall or something. And hey, you can come visit."

"I guess," I said, and lifted my shoulder to run my cheek down it. It felt good to touch the soft skin on the inside of my arm.

"You could even move there, Pretty," she said in a nice way. "You'd fit right in." She smiled at me, nudged my arm. "Girl, you could be out and proud."

The waitress came over, and Jamie ordered some banana pudding to go for her papaw.

I picked at a scab on my fat knuckle and shrugged. "Proud of what?"

***

A few days later Jamie texted me and said she was going to quit Food Country and go look at apartments. She and her boyfriend were in a real hurry to get moved. She said she'd swing by the store the morning before they left so she could say hey to me and put in her notice. When checkers put in notice at Food Country, they get wiped off the schedule so they don't steal money out of their registers on their last day. So that was going to be it for Jamie, and we both knew it.

I didn't want to see her. I thought about it all night while the neighbors hollered on their porch and threw beer bottles at our windows. I listened through the wall to my dad snoring in the next room, thought about how nobody would pick up that dead bear, and decided I didn't want to let myself look at Jamie even one more time. I didn't sleep much.

The next morning, her boyfriend's jeep pulled up around eleven and sat idling in front of the cart rack at the main entrance. Before she got out, Jamie kissed him a bunch of times, right there by the big store windows. *She's so cool and beautiful*, I thought. She wasn't ever gonna stay here. I should have known that.

She started to climb out of the jeep to come inside, and my knees buckled. All I knew was, I didn't want to hear her say she was quitting. I pulled out my register key and shuffled quick to the back of the store. Let her talk to Carter. Travis. Anybody. Shit.

In the back, I didn't know where to hide that she wouldn't come looking for me. All I could think was to go in Fuckface's office. Nobody ever went in there. I bolted straight for the door that said "MANAGER," squeaked inside, saw an old green filing cabinet, and ducked behind it. I crouched low with my head down in my hands and sat there a long time.

After a few minutes, I heard Carter's voice say, "Uh, sir? Have you seen that girl Pretty, the one with the buzz cut?"

I looked up. Fuckface was at his big metal manager's desk, looking right at me. Carter was on the other side of the cabinet and couldn't see me. Fuckface just stared. His eyes always looked kind of bugged, so it probably didn't seem strange to Carter, but I thought he was going to shoot lasers at me out of those eyes. They were bright blue. It freaked me out.

Fuckface turned his head toward Carter, but he kept looking at me. Then he said, real soft, "Check the walk-in fridges. I don't want her smoking that contraption of hers in there."

I heard Carter say, "Yes, sir," and I thought I heard the tapping of another pair of feet. Jamie must have been with him, wanting to talk to me.

After they left, I whispered, "I couldn't. I just couldn't." I whispered it to Fuckface. And I sat there behind the cabinet for another half hour. He never said a word.

***

Eventually, Fuckface got up from his desk and grabbed his keys, took his wallet out of a drawer. Lunchtime. He gave me a quick glance while he straightened his shiny tie, and I watched him leave. After he was gone, I wriggled out from behind the cabinet and stood in his office working up the courage to go back to my register.

The manager's office was painted a sad hospital-green color. Paint chips and dirt smudges hid in all the corners. The whole place was filled with paper. It spilled everywhere. The desk had a dusty black computer on it, and it looked like Fuckface was working on about a million spreadsheets. I went around to his side of the desk and peeked. The spreadsheets were all kinds of money and product lists stacked haywire. On the monitor was a spreadsheet with all us checkers' drawer totals. He had columns for all the employees. Next to the keyboard he had printed out a master list and a few spreadsheets from previous months, all labeled at the top. On the screen and the printouts, my name had a green bar going across my totals. I figured that meant I was doing all right, because some of the other girls had yellow bars or red lines. Jamie had her name grayed out.

Underneath one spreadsheet pile was a magazine called *The Advocate*. I pushed some paper around to look at it. The cover had a picture of a skinny actor in a fancy suit. The actor had makeup on, and he was holding his collar in a real artistic way, fingers arced, long and delicate. Looking at that picture calmed me down somehow. I stared at that magazine until I heard Carter bark my name.

"Pretty. What the . . ." He was standing in the door of Fuckface's office. He looked at me like he'd never seen me before. Then he sighed a long breath. "Jamie quit."

I nodded and ran my fingers over the magazine. The cover felt so smooth, and I wondered where Fuckface had got it from. We didn't sell magazines like that here. My eyes started to go fuzzy, and my face went hot.

"Go on out back and take a break," Carter muttered.

I sniffed and nodded, and he left me alone.

I went to the back door and opened it quiet. I eased outside and reached in my pocket for my vape. Before I headed to the picnic table, I looked to my left, prepared for the sight of rotting bear. I couldn't help it; we had grown used to having it there with us. It was part of my routine now, and in a weird way, I wanted to see the bear this time.

Fuckface was at the edge of the back lot standing over the carcass. His legs were parted, and he was holding a big, rusty shovel I'd never seen before. His jaw was clenched up tight, and even though I barely knew him, I could tell he was pissed. I didn't move.

On the ground next to the bear was a big blue tarp laid out flat. Using the shovel like a lever, Fuckface rolled the body onto the tarp a little bit at a time until it was just barely over the edge. Then he grabbed the tarp and pulled up slow with both hands. He rolled the bear in further to the middle, and its head turned over twice. It was just a big old cub, a yearling. It had probably wandered and got spooked, caught in traffic. I felt bad for its momma. Its tongue stuck out, dark brown and stiff, and its big, awkward feet were crumpled and broken like they'd been run over. One front paw was bent backward over itself.

Fuckface folded the tarp over the body real careful until it looked like a big, sad burrito. He knelt down. He put his right hand on top of the blue lump with the bear inside, right on top of it, like a preacher would lay hands on a sinner. He thought about something for a long minute, but his lips didn't move. I leaned against the back wall of the store and watched him.

I'd never had occasion to notice before, but it turned out Fuckface had a lot of muscles. We don't look at him much. After he took his hand off the tarp, he knelt down tighter and put his arms under the bundle he'd made and lifted that bear up like it was nothing. His silver pickup was right behind him with the gate down. That bear looked heavy—a hundred pounds easy. Fuckface's muscles strained and bulged under his gray slacks as he lifted the bear. His arms and shoulders were huge, and it occurred to me maybe my manager got more done around the store than we gave him credit for. He was big enough, and he had all those spreadsheets. He didn't have to hide.

He turned and hauled the tarp into his truck in one clean motion. The bear made a hard thud when it landed. The truck bounced, and the thud echoed so sharp it felt like a punch to my chest. Fuckface sat on the edge of his truck bed for about two seconds, then he whacked his fingers against his leg and stood. He slammed the truck's gate closed, then he turned and found the old shovel on the ground. He grabbed it in one hand, gripped it firm, walked to the edge of the back lot, and slung the shovel into the weeds.

On the way back to his truck he caught me looking at him. Our eyes met, and Fuckface nodded at me, sharp and quick. He stood still for a second with his head down, and then he put his left hand out toward me. Not pointing exactly, and not waving. It was like he was signaling me, but I didn't know what his hand was trying to say, so I stayed where I was until he lowered it back down again. Then he turned, climbed in his truck, and drove off.

I stood there a long time wondering where Fuckface would dump that yearling. Maybe I should have offered to help him find somewhere peaceful to take it, but I couldn't clear the distance. I couldn't just get in somebody's truck like that. Then I went to the empty picnic table with my vape. While I smoked, I hummed one of the Joan Armatrading songs Jamie had played me a few times—something about mining for gold in dim places.

I sat out there behind Food Country for most of the afternoon, staring into the weeds behind the store, at the mountains beyond, trying to figure out a way to keep living here without going crazy. I puffed my vape and wondered about Fuckface a little, about his weird magazines and spreadsheets and management style, but mostly I just thought about how bad I wanted to sleep someplace quiet at night. The whole day went loose and cloudy after that.

Later that night I lay in bed with my eyes squeezed closed, and I pictured Jamie wearing lots of bright rings and stones. Everything in my picture looked far from me, close to her. I didn't know how to reach out and grab onto stuff the way Jamie did. Maybe if somebody could wrap me up in a big, blue tarp and take me into the forest someplace, that would fix things. Outside, the mountains hung low and mean in every direction. The walls of the trailer rattled in time with the neighbors' music, and not a thing in the world held any light in the dark.

BOOMER

By the time May took the frog lamps, Larry was losing Hollow Rock. First she took the big stuff—loveseat, dining table, three bookshelves. When it was just state forest service guys like himself putting out small brush fires, before the election, before everything burned or surrendered, there had still been dishes in the cabinets.

The first of October was warm. This time, when May said again marriage wasn't worth it, they ought to just hang it up, instead of punching walls, Larry nodded.

All right, May belle, he said. Then that's what we'll do.

May didn't understand. You want me to go?

You've been trying to go a long time, Larry said.

She blinked. What would I do?

Whatever you want, Larry said. Don't take care of me.

May narrowed her eyes. What is wrong with you?

A lot I reckon, Larry said.

May repeated each question, rewording each time. Larry answered the same.

The next morning he got called in to assist a team on the Qualla Boundary with a quick-spreading fire close to state lands. Some kids had left a cookout that caught brush. Up north, twelve wildfires had already started. Larry scowled into his phone and watched amateur videos posted from Kentucky. He drove out into Cherokee tribal lands and spent two days stopping the cookout fire before it seeped into virgin forest. The Qualla crew was spooked.

It better rain, they said.

Larry and four Cherokee fighters gathered on the ridge above the campground. They assessed, checked for smoke. They looked down into the narrow valley where tourists teemed every autumn. Fudge shops, neon tomahawks. Summer had been a long drought, five states wide, and October was coming in clear and mild. It hadn't rained for seven weeks, and none was forecast. The NOAA alerts out of Asheville kept using the word "unprecedented."

Leaf season's no good without a little rain, they said. No color.

One wiry ranger squatted in the leaves.

We're lucky we caught this when we did, he said. Whole place could go up.

The Cherokee were well equipped—casino money and federal grants made it easy to get things under control there. The tribe's firehouse had a pizza oven and Wi-Fi. Larry slept in his truck both nights, even though he didn't have to. He dreamed about May. The news and firehouse chatter were all election talk, and he didn't want to listen. Larry felt weighted down, as if somehow the news, the Qualla fire, his troubles with May had all been his fault. So he made some silence for himself. Inside the quiet of his truck he pondered everything May had grumbled, everything they'd agreed to.

He wondered how it would feel to live alone, to lose out.

When he got home from Qualla, ragged and sore and reeking of smoke, May wouldn't let him in the house.

You stink, she said. Stay out here and clean off.

The rays of wrinkles around her eyes had deepened.

You got somebody, she said. Who is she?

She isn't, he said. It's just me. Nobody else.

So you're just going to live here by yourself? We're both going to be alone?

I thought you wanted to be alone, he said. I thought I was letting you go.

May smirked.

You never let me do anything, she said.

Larry stood on the porch. His rucksack slumped against a post, and a tube of Bengay peeked out from his T-shirt pocket. He squatted, dug around in his rucksack, and pulled out three pairs of wet, filthy socks. He flung them over the white porch railing. They hung limp and gray like rotting game skins.

I'm moving over to my sister's, May told him through the screen door. I'm not staying in this old place. You can have it.

Larry nodded. He looked across the yard, up the dirt road to the swell of mountain behind his land, and pulled the Bengay out of his pocket like he was cupping a moth. The trees twinkled amber, gold. He didn't mention it wasn't her house to give. He was a Helm County native. His grandfather built this place, and Larry had whitewashed its sides and cut the grass since he was nine. May's name wasn't on the deed.

I'll get a job, May said.

Larry shook a crust of mud off his left boot and told her that was good.

I wouldn't be doing it for you, May said.

She crossed her arms and stared at him as he screwed open the tube and put the cap on the railing. Her body was elfin, her jaw a triangle. She tilted her head sideways until her chin pointed toward Larry's socks. As she cocked her head, a shiny blue glass earring appeared from behind her hair. She didn't ask about the fire.

May stood between the screen door and the oak front door, head to the side, blue glass catching light, and watched him work salve into his arms. The television bickered in the living room—one of the news channels. Her body blocked some of the arguments roiling out of the speakers, but the voices still carried and rattled Larry's teeth.

He's gonna win, May said, closing her eyes. That pig. Listen to him.

Larry told her to turn it off.

May flitted into the house and slammed the front door. He pulled a towel off the plastic laundry rack at the edge of the porch. He wiped his face, sank into a deck chair, and let his arms hang limp. The Bengay's mentholated tang seeped into his muscles while he stared at the woodpile under the carport.

A flick of russet darted across the top of the woodpile and wiggled between two hunks of pine. Larry leaned forward. A few seconds later the red flicker appeared again. Boomer squirrel. He was little and twitchy, all red fur, with short tufts sprouting from each ear. Larry liked red squirrels. They weren't fat or mean like grays. Boomers had spirit, and he could swear they winked at you sometimes.

The boomer flashed around some more, then darted up the hickory near the mailbox. He was making ready for winter, stashing most of his nuts and treats in the woodpile. Larry muttered to the squirrel as it scurried. It should have been hiding its food elsewhere; the woodpile was a bad spot, a temporary structure. Soon the boomer would lose his stores to Larry's woodstove.

Better to bury in the ground, little buddy, he said. Better to keep up in the trees.

He stayed on the porch and watched afternoon light glow through the hickory trees while May thundered inside the house. The television stayed on, pundits on low boil. He checked his phone for updates, texted colleagues. He'd have to go back out soon; smoke reports were coming faster, and yellow bubbles of text popped brightly on his screen. Tellico. Ferebee. High spots, far from each other. National forest, too. Nantahala was smoldering.

May burst out of the front door holding a purple end table.

She'd painted it in a crafting class at the Folk Center a couple years back.

I'm taking this, she said.

She stomped down the porch steps, turned back.

I'll need furniture, she said. You've never given me a thing.

He eased himself up to a stand. He was six four, built thick and gingery, and he had just gone forty last spring. May crunched her sandaled feet across the gravel drive and popped the trunk on her hatchback. Larry kneaded the back of his neck, went inside, and slept in a dark coma for seventeen hours.

***

A few days later, all of Helm County was put under a Severe Threat. Larry wanted to file a report to Raleigh about Qualla. Nobody was paying attention to the campfire bans; nobody was talking about Kentucky. The state office needed to get their act together; a new parks secretary might be appointed in January, depending on how the votes shook out, so bureaucrats were hibernating under their log books until then.

Ten thousand acres in Georgia had already burned. Twenty thousand in Virginia. The problem was getting worse, spreading, closing in on Helm County, on the whole state, from north and south.

Hollow Rock, ten miles from his house, backed up onto fifteen square miles of usually damp, lush state forest. That whole expanse was a husk. Hollow Rock was more corkscrew than mountain—a massive, undulating mound of earth that separated the tourist hamlet of Chimney Gap from the state lands encircling Helm County. If any fire leaked out of Hollow into the state forest, or vice versa, it would do so in a mean spiral. Every ridge would burn, and so would the town. Everybody Larry knew would lose their home.

Locals were calling 911 to report smoke here and there, tiny blazes or yard burns that town firefighters dutifully quashed. The forest floor rustled itself in even the weakest breeze. Fluffed-up leaves, all papery and loose, waited to catch light. Larry thought it was as if the whole of the world was asking to be fuel. The air snapped with brittle coolness and smelled of rust.

We need to dig some lines, Larry's guys said. Need to get those helicopters in from Tennessee.

Some of his state forest service team were close to retirement, others still green and young. Larry fell about in the middle, in terms of experience.

They're federal, the longtimers said. They got the resources. Those choppers need to be here. We're worse off than anybody.

Larry nodded, even though he believed everywhere from West Virginia to Georgia was the worst off any place could possibly be.

The team muttered to each other, counted out locations and shifts with their thick fingers.

Preventive measures, they said. While we still can.

***

By mid-October, he had forgotten what day it was. He forgot about Qualla and Raleigh. He stayed in Helm County, kept an eye on Hollow Rock. His team set prescribed burns. They pulled back tons of underbrush, cleared out the carpet of leaf litter and ripe tinder from miles of home ground. Masks covered their faces, so they spent entire days, in woods they had hunted since childhood, nodding and signaling to each other like pitchers and catchers.

Sparks multiplied. Larry worked. Above Highway 9 a few miles from his house, he helped cut dozer lines in the dusty earth to stop the front marching down from the north. He corralled volunteers, surveyed, soaked the ground. In between prevention efforts, state park dispatch, tower lookouts, 911, and his own instinct took him to fires all over the county. Some were weeks-old lightning strikes that waited, burning slow, gaining power on the still-damp ridgetops. Elsewhere a devil set them. After Christmas they would arrest some whack job arsonist who set at least twenty fires on purpose, but nobody knew that yet. Most of the problem was stray cigarette butts or people burning yard waste without a permit, without sense. It wasn't something local folks had ever worried about before. They were used to morning dews and soaking rains and black, moist loam.

Blazes foomed up like signals from the peaks, and the sky for fifty miles in any direction was a low tarp of ash. Volunteers streamed in, and October tumbled quietly out of control. The governor released the National Guard. FEMA set up evacuation stations up and down the Blue Ridge. A bunch of fighters from out west trucked themselves to Hollow Rock. They were returning a kindness from two years ago, when southern firefighters had helped save half of Oregon.

None of this made the news.

When he could get away, Larry would drive home, shower, eat, crash. In his sleep he heard the thrum of helicopters making retardant drops.

The first thing he noticed missing was the sofa. He came out of the bathroom and stood naked and soggy in the living room and felt a weird, unfamiliar breeze to his right. It took him a moment to look in that direction and realize she'd taken it. Larry wondered which of May's friends owned a pickup, how she'd wrestled the loveseat's puffy, awkward body out the narrow door. She was so small. A few days later the bed in the spare room was missing, and there were no plates or bowls to eat off of. May was emptying him out.

He switched from day shifts and went out in the night. Not that it mattered; either way he was gone for days at a time. He saw less and less of May, who still did not ask about the fires. He slept while she was awake; he fought fire while she slept.

Night work suited him. He could see the enemy and nothing else; he could focus. Larry fought for Hollow Rock every night through November. The teams were just barely staying ahead of the threats, which were legion, fierce, and scattered. First they prayed for rain. When rain didn't come, they prayed for smoke, the death of wind, a cold fog to choke oxygen, douse sparks. Instead, the clear fall weather gave the blazes air, feeding every small hell. The forest went cinematic at night, with lit slithers of amber inching in chiaroscuro through the trees and blackness.

Millions of orange cinders floated around Larry perpetually in the dark. Fire likes to jump, to send out emissaries. Each night, more ignited dander and duff—leaves, twigs, campsite detritus—swirled and arced over the ditches they dug and above the pocked, disused logging roads they used as markers, lines of defense. Embers burned bright and small, like sprites carrying the news of fire. Larry watched them with his mouth open. He wheezed inside his mask; his breaths echoed and pooled hotly on his upper lip. Even masked, he could taste the firebrands in the scorched air. They were lighted wicks uncandled, unbound tendrils eating themselves. They passed delicately in front of him, seeking hosts, filling his view as they yearned across every thwarting gap. When it was quiet, when no one was shouting, Larry heard the trees recoil. Branches crackled; trunks creaked and flinched from the bite of flame.

Most of the embers burned themselves out, dissipating into charred vapor. Some he swatted or stomped. The ones he couldn't reach, the few that caught a wind, continued on in the thick ether, above the forest, eventually coming to rest on fresh, dry victims in the distance.

***

In November a fire behaviorist came down from Virginia to direct a controlled burn near the Chimney Gap golf course. They wanted to save the condos and rental cabins, so Larry and the Oregon team filled driptorches and lit up stands of cedars on the back nine. The behaviorist said it would stop the skulking blazes from coming over the hills and taking out residential buildings. Starve the worst fronts, stall the rate of spread. It would spare the east side of town, the behaviorist told the club manager, who fretted over the grand, older oaks that lined the fairways.

Kill a margin, said the behaviorist, for the greater good.

Larry, the behaviorist, and a dozen Oregonians led by a burly woman named Link spent two days on the burn. When it was over, a prophylactic line of char was established across the perimeter of the country club. Link's team roamed the cauterized stripe of land afterward. They checked for sparks, scarred their boots, stood dazed in the carnage. Some of the Oregonians fell asleep leaning against their trucks. Others roamed the blackline still holding driptorches, which puffed contained flame from thick metal tips. Occasionally someone would unleash a torch into a tangle of brush they'd missed. Twigs and bushes plumed in round, silent explosions.

In the evening of the second day, the behaviorist stood beside Larry atop a steep hillside crawling with fire. The hilltop looked out over the state forest into distant, peaceful blue ridgelines. Below burned the worst of Helm County's trouble. The sun set quickly, and snakes of flame downhill churned in an early twilight, moving upward toward their blackline.

The behaviorist was bald, fifty, militaristic. His name was Don. Pale and thick in the shoulders, he could have been Larry's kin. They looked down and watched the front approach. Punches of heat seeped toward them. Larry had taken off his turnout gear and tossed it in a nearby truck. He fumbled with his suspenders and T-shirt, wiped sweat from under his eyes. His eyelashes were singed and uneven. Black particulate sprinkled his brow and made gray streaks in his chin stubble.

Look at it, Don the behaviorist said.

A snow of ash hung around them in the sharp air.

Get the hoses, Larry said.

Link and two Oregonians dragged themselves up and set to work. Don sniffed and shook his head slowly.

It's not going to rain tomorrow, he said. They said it might, but it won't. I don't think it ever will.

Larry squatted and stared down the writhing, glowing slope. Behind him, to the west, a breeze came across the fairway, cooling the blackline and tickling his back. It wafted past the trucks, past Link's crew, over his body. It cooled his skin and pushed back the scent of smoke; then it blew through the fading sunlight and floated, thoughtlessly, carelessly, down the mountainside, down into the gloom and the rising heat.

Blazing tendrils of ladder fire, a full-on front burning from root to kudzu to canopy, fed themselves on that wind. The flames suckled for it, raged like addicts. Remnants of twilight purpled the Oregonians' skin as Larry watched the updrafts gorge themselves on air.

Larry and Don stood on their blackened swath worrying into the abyss. The trees here were all networked into each other, a thick hash of enmeshed twig and vine. A low blanket of merciful smoke might have stifled what was coming. But the breeze came again, blithe and fresh, and the scene burned bright and hellish.

This is what happens, said Don.

Larry squatted, pulled a hunk of beef jerky out of his pocket. The meat was a wilted, hot lump of putty.

Y'all should have done more land use planning, said Don. More management.

They cut our budget, Larry said. They cut it every year.

Same in Virginia. Same everywhere, said Don. Plus, perfect conditions. It's a bad fall.

I feel responsible, Larry said.

You didn't light the match, said Don.

I didn't mind the matchbook, either, Larry said.

If this breeze keeps up, we'll get a stack effect, said Don. That's gonna be bad.

Larry chewed his jerky and nodded once, slow.

There's too many cultivated species here, said Don, twisting toward the golf course. He pointed his clipboard at the ridge above town.

Up there? he said. You got native trees. Just looking for a reason to burn.

Look who you're telling, Larry said.

They both stared down the slope again, into the coming fire. Heat pushed against them and oiled their skin.

Hell, said Don, we earned it. This whole damn business. We brought it out.

They waited for Link to bring the hoses. She knew what to do.

***

His negotiations with May had looped and replayed all through the weeks of burning. If Larry was home, she asked the same questions. Called him a son of a bitch. Couldn't make sense of it. Each time May spun faster, flipped her oak-colored hair, and parried with more logic. She was looking for reasons, for names. Larry didn't know how to tell her there was no reason. He didn't know how to tell her the world was just ending; that was all.

She made Larry sit down the day she packed up her clothes. It was four in the afternoon, and he'd just woken up. May's nose barely came to his chest. It was cold out, and she had taken most of what she wanted. She sat him on a footstool in the empty kitchen. She stood, brown eyes flickering, hips at a slant. The house had now fully absorbed the sweet smell of burnt forest that Larry kept bringing home with him. It was a heavy odor, thick as pine sap in the air between them.

This is it, she said. I'll be gone day after tomorrow. Her fingernails plucked at the "I'm With Her" sticker on her water bottle.

I don't know what to say, Larry told her. I'm sorry.

***

Two days later, the Folk Center caught fire and had to be evacuated.
May heard it on the radio and stilled. She waited for Larry to get
home.

Can I have the frog lamps, she said.

Her voice was low, half tender. She was holding one of the
lamps. Her little hand cupped the pewter lily pad at its base. Her
other hand gripped its stem, a slim, iridescent column of crystal.
The stem legs swooped up into a bulbous top—a brittle, delicate
frog body leaping toward a fringed tapestry shade. The frog caught
the overhead kitchen light, refracted it. Its stomach swirled a kalei-
doscope of aquamarine hues onto May's small knuckles.

Larry was eating soup straight out of the can. He stood at the
kitchen counter with his back to her.

I'm asking, Larry. Your mom bought these for us at the Folk
Center, she said. Remember?

He leaned into the counter. The edge of the Formica cut sharply
into his hip, and he closed his eyes. He rolled a salty potato on his
tongue and wished he could go back to October, back to Qualla.
Back to the wet spring.

I want the pair, she said. They have to match. They'll be worth
something now.

Larry had spent the last thirty-six hours with a handful of Link's
crew high above Hollow Rock, in a clearing he'd never seen before.
They had been digging a broad, hopeless ditch. A platoon of nervous elk clustered at the edge of the clearing and snuffled at the
fighters while they worked. The cow elks fidgeted. The bulls folded
their legs underneath themselves and huddled in the dry leaves,
watching for hours, until the tiny herd finally rose together and
receded into the hazy wood.

Larry's hands were black. He was on his fourth pair of boots.
November was half over, and the woodpile under the carport was
shrinking as the cold set in. Only local news vans dotted the street
outside the fire station in town. All the state officials down in

Raleigh were still hoping for recounts or high-fiving each other over electoral college votes. No one knew they were here. This fire was a secret, Larry figured, some kind of evil the world was keeping from itself.

In the living room, an acorn from the boomer's stash popped inside the woodstove's iron belly. Another one pinged against the stove wall, sharp and clear. The red squirrel hadn't been around for weeks. Maybe he had moved his supplies elsewhere, like May. Or maybe he had given up and settled his squirrel brain on hunger, on letting it burn.

Rain would not come. Another blaze rising out of Transylvania would soon join theirs, doubling the conflagration. In Tennessee, people were dying, suffocating in their cars as they tried to escape. That, at least, had made the papers, alongside all the stories blaming mountain people for picking the president. Larry didn't know anyone who'd had time to vote.

Larry's lips were so chapped and raw, flakes of skin hung like torn plaster from his mouth. His fingers were so sore he couldn't ball a weak fist. He couldn't think of a place he loved or knew as a boy that wasn't on fire. His clothes, his hair, his truck, everything he owned stunk of rank sweat and ash.

Can I have them both, May said. I know you're tired, Larry. But I have to ask.

He put down his soup spoon. He turned to May and put a hand under her jaw. Her skin felt warm. His arms were weights.

Take the lamps, he told her.

The woodstove pinged again, and he breathed into May's clean hair.

Take them and whatever else, he said. Just please, honey, go on.

WIRELESS

The Holiday Inn Express on Richland Skyway seemed like as good a place as any for Margaret Price to maybe, possibly, stick her finger up a guy's butthole. At least somebody had asked her to. People didn't ask Margaret for anything, let alone sex stuff.

Margaret's sister Julie got asked out by men all the time, and people were always calling her for recipes and beauty tips. Men probably wanted Julie to do all kinds of things to their assholes. One time Julie even got asked to model for a lingerie ad in the *Lexington Herald-Leader*, but Julie declined because her ex-husband Parker would get jealous. Besides Parker, her sister could pretty much say no to whomever she pleased, and people would keep on asking. Men, everybody.

Her whole life, Margaret watched Julie field requests, yes-ing and no-ing however suited her, and she wondered what it was like to be so spoiled for choice. For Margaret, this butt-fingering question was a real opportunity, so she wanted to make sure she handled it right.

How it happened was, Margaret went to her fifteen-year reunion and bumped into Robbie Barnwell. After work on a Saturday, after Julie reminded her a dozen times, she put on a dress that felt papery from being so rarely worn, and she drove to the First Baptist Church's fellowship hall across from Bentley High School. She only went to stop Julie dogging her, to say she'd survived. And maybe, just a little, she wanted to see if anybody bothered to notice her.

Margaret parked her dinky silver Honda in the church parking lot—a seamless, fresh layer of black tar. The fellowship hall was barnlike, fifty yards from the church at the back of the lot. A church hall wasn't the kind of place Price girls frequented. She did not stop to make herself a name tag at the welcome table out front.

The inside of First Baptist's fellowship hall was a sad draggle of metal folding chairs and wood paneling under a high ceiling. Someone merciful had switched off the fluorescent lights that usually blared down on the beige carpet. The place was dim. About fifty people roamed the room smiling and pulling at suit jackets, winding necklaces around fingers. Occasionally a squeal firecrackered above the music, and everyone would turn to see two people embracing. Other than that, nobody seemed to know where to look, so they clutched their beverages and stared at the children's art taped along the walls. It was summer, so VBS kids were spending half-days making collages of the Last Supper out of construction paper and glitter. Each interpretation was a little messier than the last as the artists' ages descended in a line down the wall, from tween to preschooler.

Margaret slunk along the periphery until she came to a snack table in the back corner by a big rectangular window. Someone handed her a paper plate, which she gripped two-handed. She noted a few faces she recognized, then looked out the window at her car. She decided she would go home in exactly eleven minutes, which she began to count off in her head in sets of twenty seconds.

She had nearly reached the end of the second minute when a voice beside her said, "Well, hey there, Margaret Price."

Robbie Barnwell was scooping punch into a red plastic cup right next to her. She recognized him immediately and felt no shock, as if he were a landmark she passed every day on her way to work.

"Hey, Robbie," she said.

They got to talking, and Margaret asked about Trina Bagshot, whom Robbie had married right after high school.

"She's all right," Robbie said. "Working for the state now. Child services."

"Y'all still together?" She didn't ask with any hope. She was just asking.

The snack table was covered in white paper and laden with pretzel sticks and fruit trays. A sagging blue banner above them said "*Welcome Home Mustangs.*" Margaret and Robbie had been decent friends all through school. Never beat each other up, never kissed. Helped each other pass algebra. There was mutual respect.

"Fourteen years," said Robbie. His shoulders tensed under his shirt.

"Kids?" said Margaret. She looked at Robbie's thick red beard and hair, trying to remember if he'd always had that coloring. Margaret hadn't kept in touch with school friends. She had moved to Knoxville right after graduation and stayed there up until last fall, working in IT for the city's convention center. In all those years she'd probably thought about Robbie Barnwell a total of seven times, and in her mind he always had blond hair and a dead front tooth. He looked pretty good now, compared to her memory.

"Just one," said Robbie. He fished out his phone and showed her a picture of a lanky kid holding a soccer ball. A woman's arm was wrapped around the kid's skinny shoulders, and Margaret thought she recognized Trina's wide, duck-bill fingernails. She had always envied girls with nice fingernails. "He's gonna be thirteen."

"My nieces are littler than that," she said.

Somebody announced a quilt raffle to benefit the marching band, and the music switched to an old song about not wanting it to rain.

"What about you? You get married or anything?"

Margaret looked around the fellowship hall, past her peers from the Class of '97, out the window. This time she looked past her car to their old high school across the road. A new baseball field was being gouged out of the south hillside, and the lowering sun glowed on the diggers and culvert pipe. She hated that old lump of earth. For decades the little hill between the school and the woods had been a mucky, dark tumor. It was the one spot no one could see from any classroom windows. The south hillside had been, in her day, the territory of bullies and potheads, a whole mess of never for any vulnerable kid. She hadn't set foot on that soil since junior year, and she never would again. Julie had been the one to tell her they were bulldozing it. Sounded good to Margaret.

According to Julie, they were using the baseball field funds to lay fiber optic cables around the school, bury the power lines. Bentley, Kentucky, was modernizing. The clay under the moved earth of the south hill was raw, russet, almost bloodred.

Margaret knew Robbie knew she wasn't married. Everybody knew, but it was nice of him to ask. Margaret shook her head in answer to his question.

"Well, you look good. You seeing anybody?"

Margaret shrugged. "I just focused on my career."

Robbie sipped punch, nodded and laughed. "Yeah, you definitely weren't the Redneck Stepford type."

It was the nicest way anybody in Bentley had ever called Margaret a freak. Which she was. Always, from the time she was little, Margaret had felt off-kilter in the scrubbed respectability of this place. The few friends she'd had had all been kids from the coal camps or foster care. To this day, everybody of significance in Bentley treated Margaret like the spare button on the inside of a shirt. But here Robbie was, acknowledging her strangeness as a matter of course, without pity or derision.

She turned toward him and handed him a small square napkin. He had punch on his cuff.

Robbie dotted the stain. "Your parents still liking Florida?"

"They've got a condo near the water. High on the hog."

"What about you?" Robbie said. "You sure left town in a hurry after school. Making good money down there in Knoxville?"

"Nope," said Margaret.

He held his cup halfway to his mouth and gave her an eyebrow. "You get fired?"

"I quit," said Margaret. "Came back home last fall, when Julie's divorce was final. She asked me to come help out with my nieces for a little while, and I wound up staying. You remember my sister?"

"Sure, I remember Julie."

He didn't smile or say the name with any energy, and Margaret felt her abs loosen. He wasn't going to ask how Julie was, if she was still a looker, all the questions men usually had. He didn't care about her sister. Julie wasn't the reason Robbie was talking to Margaret. They were just talking, like they used to in algebra class.

"Anyhow, now I manage the GameStop on Richland Skyway." Margaret felt like she had to explain that last part, so she picked up a cheese blob on a toothpick and added, "I stopped giving a shit about a lot of stuff a while back."

Robbie was wearing a bright blue dress shirt, no tie. "I know the feeling," he said, and looked at her. He looked Margaret right in the eye. "I didn't get a fancy career or anything. I'm just like the song."

It was Margaret's turn for an eyebrow.

"Electrician." He laughed again. "I am a lineman for the coun-teee." He put a little music at the end. "Well, kind of. I mostly do power line maintenance. All I did was get hairier. You haven't changed a bit."

Margaret smiled at Robbie. She hadn't done that to anybody in a while.

"Ain't we a pair?" he said.

***

Julie was two years older, but she remembered Robbie as soon as Margaret mentioned seeing him at the reunion. Margaret stopped by Julie's almost every day, though lately her visits had become more sporadic. Julie nudged for details, so Margaret filled her in. Everybody was just as full of shit as they were in high school, but cloudier somehow. Out of focus, she said. Except Robbie.

"Robbie Barnwell. Well, sure," Julie said. "How *is* he?"

She was wearing a slinky beige dress that matched her tan skin. Her toenails were freshly painted, and she was packing little lavender superhero suitcases for her twin girls, Eva and Grace. Margaret's nieces were nine, and they were going to a slumber party so momma could have a date night with "Uncle Jack." Jack was Julie's latest boyfriend. Margaret had promised to drive the girls to their friend's house after work.

While Julie clicked around in her new snakeskin stilettos, Margaret glared at herself in the hall mirror. She fluffed her hair and tried to pout, but she couldn't hold the pose. She and Julie had the same dark hair, same build, but Margaret's edges looked rounder, less formed. Makeup made her face feel sticky, and her shoes didn't snap when she walked. Upstairs, the girls' footfalls and giggles rumbled like a coming storm.

"He seemed good," Margaret said.

Julie breezed past her to the banister and singsong-hollered up at the girls not to keep Auntie waiting. Then she turned back and straightened a family portrait hanging in the hallway. The frame held Julie, the girls, and Julie's ex-husband Parker Hackett in a permanent cuddle. They all wore matching blue turtlenecks, and behind them, autumn mountains blazed. The frame never hung straight on its nail.

"Why don't you take that picture down?" Margaret asked as

Julie breezed past again. "It's creepy. At least put it in the girls' room."

Julie's step hitched. She looked over her shoulder and flamingoed her legs. "I can't," she said, one hand on the doorframe. "It wouldn't be right. Parker would notice when he comes by."

"Who gives a shit?"

"He'll be here Wednesday," Julie said. "To see them."

"What, in the middle of the week? How come?"

"There's a school thing. It's—just a thing."

"Fine," said Margaret. "Note to self: do not visit Wednesday."

Julie's feet sputtered, but soon both heels were clicking across the kitchen floor again. Margaret followed her, admiring the way the stiletto straps wisped around Julie's ankles. She reached the line of four barstools facing the sink and leaned on one.

"Did you know Robbie Barnwell has red hair?" she asked.

Her sister scrunched her brow and bobbed her head. She folded a white cloth and wiped down a glistening granite countertop that didn't need wiping.

"I guess?" said Julie. "Didn't he marry Trina Bagshot?"

"They got divorced," said Margaret.

She edged onto a stool and stared hard at Julie, waiting to see if she'd be caught in the lie.

Julie bent down and grabbed the mini-suitcases. She flopped them on the counter between her and Margaret. "Well," she said with a wide, whitened smile.

"What?"

"Well, there you go!" said Julie, waving at her. Her gold bracelet sparkled in the light.

"Jesus, Julie. I'll probably never see him again."

Margaret put her elbow on the cool granite and kicked her sneaker against the underside of the bar. Julie rested her hand on the nearest suitcase and took a long breath.

"The girls' teacher said they've loaned out all the books you donated for the Reading Marathon," Julie said. "Asked if you could send more. But"—she wrinkled her nose—"nothing else with robots or scary centaurs or, you know, apocalypses."

"But those are the best ones," Margaret said. She had pulled a toppling stack of childhood favorites out of the old boxes in Julie's attic for the Reading Marathon. She hoped the kids read every single apocalypse.

"They're still little," her sister said.

"So?"

"So Pauline Hardwick told me her son was reading about some pirate being guillotined."

"That," said Margaret, tapping a finger, "is a damn fine story."

Julie rolled her eyes and shook her head. "They're *nine*, Peg."

"I know—" Margaret's head shot up. "The hell? Don't call me that."

Peg was what people called her when she was a kid. Peg was short for Margaret, and she hated it. It made her sound like a piece of wood. Like a rag doll. It made her feel tiny, and senior year of high school she had quit answering to it until everyone started using her full name.

"Sorry. I'm just . . ." Julie tapped a toe.

Margaret glared at her sister and tried to remember the last time she'd used her former nickname.

"It's nice you saw Robbie," said Julie. She straightened her back and grinned. "Everybody's getting divorced now," she said brightly. She checked the zipper on one of the suitcases. "You might catch somebody on the second round!"

Margaret squinted. "Where the hell did 'Peg' come from?"

Julie started to make a meek sound, but it got drowned out by Eva and Grace tumbling down the stairs. The girls fell all over Margaret. She scooped their skinny, wiggly girl bodies out to her Honda and pretended she didn't see Julie biting her cheek as she waved goodbye. Julie always said Margaret would get noticed more by men if she'd make a little effort, but Margaret didn't want to be noticed. She didn't want to hear old nicknames or talk about Robbie Barnwell or see pictures of dickhead Parker Hackett in her sister's goddamn hallway. She just wanted everybody to leave her alone.

***

When Robbie walked into GameStop a week later, Margaret tripped hard on an endcap and stubbed her foot so bad her eyes teared up. The whole time he talked to her, she thought she was bleeding into her sneaker. She thought she might even lose a toe.

"Hey, Robbie," she said. She was breathing hard and tried not to wheeze at him.

"Hey there." He held up a thin white box with a zombie on the cover. "My son wants this for his birthday. Is it . . . ?"

"Violent?" said Margaret. Robbie shrugged to indicate he didn't know the first thing about gaming.

"It's not bad," she said. "You want me to pick out some stuff for him?"

They wandered the store for a few minutes shopping and chatting. Robbie acted impressed at her technical knowledge. He even used the term "newfangled" when she pointed at a Bluetooth headset, more as a joke than anything; his truck outside was full of sensors and gadgets. Margaret almost didn't notice how nervous she was. She almost forgot about her bloody, mangled toe—which it turned out later wasn't bloody at all. Her toe was just fine. Not even bruised.

She rang Robbie up instead of letting one of her part-time clerks do it. She was bagging his son's presents when he said, "You getting off soon? Let's get a cup of coffee or something."

"I'll be done about four," she said. As simple as that.

***

They had coffee a couple of times; then he took her to supper on a Tuesday. Right after he dropped her off and she had watched his truck disappear around the corner of her condo complex, he called her.

"You don't date much, do you, Margaret?"

"Not really." She tugged on a striped curtain and watched the space between the highway and the condo office where Robbie's truck had just been. She wanted to say, *No, never. Never ever. Please, I am invisible.*

"How come?"

She could hear the wind blowing around inside the cab of his truck. He had the window down and was shouting a little.

"Do you like men?" he asked. "It doesn't matter. I'm just asking, because—well. Sorry. I shouldn't be talking to you like this."

The roar quieted on the other end of the line. He had rolled up his window. Margaret imagined his burly shoulders rotating as he shifted in his seat to hear her better.

"Hello?"

"I'm here," she said.

"Are you mad at me?"

"No, Robbie. I just . . . I'm weird, that's all."

"Yeah," he said.

"Why do you care who I'm dating?"

"I don't know," he said. "It just seems like we're still the same, you and me. Still friends. I'm just curious."

He swung by the GameStop three more times the next week. He didn't buy anything. Margaret would take a break and sit outside with him while he complained about his job or his marriage or asked her questions she didn't want to answer.

"I don't want to answer that," she finally said. Robbie had stopped by on his way home from work and wanted to know, again, whether she ever had a boyfriend in Knoxville.

Margaret stood under the store's awning and flicked her fingernails with her thumb. Robbie made her uneasy now. He looked soft. She clenched her jaw to keep from saying things to him. She wondered how often Trina and he slept together, if he liked it when they did. She asked him about the new fiber optic lines under the high school. Robbie said he didn't work on that stuff, so she asked whether it was hard to climb telephone poles, and what happened if you touched two power lines at the same time.

"Does it close the circuit?" she asked. "Would it kill you?"

Robbie said, "You ask way more questions than I do."

Margaret touched her stomach.

"Listen," he said. "How about we write to each other? You can ask me anything you want. You're good with computers. Is that easier? To talk that way, tell each other stuff?"

"You got stuff to tell me, Robbie?" she said. Robbie shook his head, tried to laugh to lighten the heavy air between them.

So they started writing. In between lunches, they wrote each other a thousand data fragments going back twenty years. A few weeks later, Robbie sent a thread of yellow chat bubbles saying he'd had a big crush on her since sixth grade, and someday, if they ever got together and made love, he wanted Margaret to stick her finger way up in his asshole.

***

He wrote all kinds of things to her, actually. Not just sex. And not right away. First they got reacquainted, and Robbie managed to get Margaret to admit she'd kind of liked him in school, too. They texted every day, which they never mentioned when they saw each other. The apps were a separate realm through which they confessed all manner of small crimes.

"I told my sister you were divorced," she messaged him. "Just for fun."

It took Robbie a while to reply.

"If only," he said.

Margaret liked the tacit agreement the technology forced on them. She liked typing simple, obvious things she didn't tell other people, like how jealous she was of Julie's clothes, or how sometimes she lied on the store's time sheets so the better clerks got paid a little extra. These electronic conversations buzzed and charged underneath their face-to-face meetings.

They used email and chat apps, three or four different methods. Robbie had a cabin near the state park where he often spent weekends with his son. There was no internet there, so it sometimes took multiple methods to reach each other. Margaret only had a vague idea where Robbie lived. She didn't know what Trina did in his absence, or what she must have thought when her husband was gone for such long periods. She decided she didn't care. Robbie was married, and Margaret didn't care.

Robbie wrote about his job. He wrote about his son, who was named Thomas and who would soon need braces. He wrote about wanting to divorce Trina, but he didn't want a bad breakup like all his friends had had, so he stuck it out. Margaret wrote about Knoxville and how she never really liked it much, how when she had come back to Bentley last fall, she was almost, almost glad to come home.

"I tell people I came back to help Julie with the girls," she messaged, "but she doesn't really need me anymore. Probably the other way around."

Somewhere in the stream of pings and notifications, Robbie began to send her his fantasies. They were tame compared to what the pimply teenagers at GameStop snorted about when the store wasn't busy. Robbie got more detailed, until finally one night while Margaret was putting a whitening strip on her teeth before bed, he emailed her a bulleted list of positions:

"69," the first bullet said.

"More face sitting," said the second one. "I've done it, but not enough."

"Tied up. Nothing kinky, no chains."

"Butt stuff . . . could be a whole sub-list. Is this weird?"

And so on.

Margaret liked the format; she liked that it was bulleted, not numbered. His desires weren't ranked, but they were organized. Clean. The cleanliness somehow absolved her of shame. She didn't say she'd do any of it. Instead she replied, "Interesting assortment," and signed off.

In her bathroom, she pulled off the whitening strips and rolled them into tiny, tight balls that she stuck on the edge of the pink washstand. She stared at them and wondered what it would be like to be with Robbie. She imagined his beard rubbing against her while she fell asleep at his cabin. The state park was mostly forest; she might hear animals or hunters in the night while she lay next to him. As she clicked off the bathroom light, she reminded herself she'd never tell a soul about their conversations. She especially wouldn't tell Julie, because that would spoil everything.

The next day Margaret felt like she owed Robbie a consolation prize for dismissing his bulleted ass-fingering list. When they met for a slushie, she could tell he was embarrassed. So that night she curled up on her sofa and wrote Robbie about how she was invisible, but really, she *did* want to be seen. She did. She just didn't know how, because of Julie, who was so much prettier and more at ease. And because of Bentley being such a conservative town, and how different she'd always felt here, and all the heaviness that never went away for her after high school the way it did for other people.

Robbie's avatar on their preferred chat app was a buck.

The buck head asked, "What kind of heaviness?"

The buck head asked, "Why do u still feel like u did in h.s.?"

The buck head blinked and waited.

But Margaret went to bed. That was as much confessing as she had in her.

The next day, Robbie brought her an iced coffee at work. They sat on his truck bumper. It was hot, and Margaret sweated under her polo. The shirt was red, with the word "Manager" embroidered over her left breast. She hoped Robbie wouldn't try to kiss her, not while she felt so sticky and gross, and not where her employees, especially pimply Caleb, who sometimes leered at her, could see.

"So," Robbie said, "what you wrote last night. Tell me what you meant." It was the first time he'd brought up something from their electronic conversations. He was breaking the rules.

Margaret scratched her head and lied, "I don't know. What'd I say?"

"High school. You said you don't like to talk about certain things." The way he said it, the tone, made Margaret think maybe Robbie already had some idea, but she couldn't name what he might have guessed. Not even to herself. That's how far down, how deep she kept it.

She shrugged and looked at her feet. "Long time ago."

"Yeah, but Margaret."

Robbie was leaning toward her. She hunched her shoulders.

"Look, all I'm gonna say is . . ." He took off his baseball cap and crossed his legs, one foot on his knee. He cocked his ear to the hum of a transformer at the edge of the parking lot. "All I'm gonna say is, Parker Hackett is a fucking asshole. Is and was."

Margaret took the words like a punch. She figured she was supposed to start crying, start wailing and show scars. Instead she laughed. Not loud, just a little snort. She waited a second to see what happened. Her chest tightened, but that was all, so she snorted again.

"No shit he is." She kept her head down. "I should know."

"Does he ever bother you?"

"No. I hardly see him. I make sure not to stop by Julie's if he's visiting the girls."

"How long those two been divorced?"

"About a year."

Robbie shook his head. "Daughters. A man like that's got two daughters," he said, and pushed his thumb hard into the sole of his work boot. "Ain't right."

"What do you know?" Margaret asked. Her voice was quiet, weak.

"I know he's a piece of shit," said Robbie. "I know he must have been a piece of shit to you. And I know you weren't the only one. Trina told me some stuff."

Margaret popped forward. "Did he do something to Trina, too?"

The "too" was out of her mouth before she realized its portent, and she blushed hot.

Robbie took a heavy breath. "He tried," he said. "Grabbed her after cheerleading practice one time and almost . . . you know. Scared her pretty bad. She had bruises, but she got away."

He looked at the traffic again. "Trina didn't tell the cops. She wishes now she had, but you know how things were back then. Nobody would've done anything. He was a quarterback."

Margaret nodded.

"I fucking hate football," said Robbie. "Hope Thomas never plays."

Margaret's memory flashed onto Parker slamming Robbie into a rank of lockers in tenth grade and calling him a pussy. She decided she hated everybody in this town except Robbie.

"Trina didn't tell me until last year, after we started marriage counseling," he said. "I was seeing this woman, and Trina found out about it, and . . . anyway. We were getting along OK; it was Thanksgiving. We were watching some show about that case in Florida. You know the swimmer, the one who got a life sentence for what he did to that girl?"

Margaret nodded.

"We got done watching, and Trina said, 'Somebody needs to do that to Parker Hackett.' I asked her what she meant, and she told me about how he attacked her."

Margaret unclenched her shoulders and put her hand on the bumper.

"Should I quit talking?" he said.

"No, I just need to stand up for a second. What else did Trina say?"

"Not much," said Robbie. He thumbed his boot again. "Just how she thought he was, you know. A predator. She was pretty sure he'd raped a couple girls. Stuff like that."

Margaret shifted her weight from one foot to the other, but she didn't move. Robbie planted his feet hard on the pavement.

"And I *knew*, Margaret. As soon as Trina told me, I realized I knew. I thought about you right away." He coughed, shifted his ass on the truck's bumper. "And you know I've got three sisters," he said. "So I'm just saying, I don't understand, but I do, kind of. From my sisters, from Trina. I think I understand."

Margaret leaned toward the door of the GameStop and measured the distance back inside. When the world didn't end, she stayed put.

"Parker was a dick to everybody. I never did like him," Robbie said. "But I didn't put the pieces together until Trina and me talked about you. She remembered how you skipped town after Julie got engaged to him."

A Harley roared past them through the intersection and rattled both their bodies.

"And then there you were," Robbie said when the bike had passed. "At the reunion. And I don't know. You made sense. After all these years, I knew what made you act weird senior year." He shrugged. "I mean, weirder than usual. It was clear as a bell when I saw you."

Margaret squeezed her drink, unsqueezed it. Squeezed it again. "I always liked Trina."

"She liked you, too. We all did." He cleared his throat.

They glanced at each other and looked away. "You ever tell the cops?"

Margaret shook her head.

"Your parents? Anybody?" he said. Margaret shrugged.

"Well," he said. "I've seen Parker a couple of times in Lexington. At that Hummer dealership on the interstate where he works. Still pulls the jock routine with me. Grown-ass man. I can't imagine what it must have been like for you while he was married to Julie. Jesus."

"I wasn't around," she said. "I left. I didn't come back here till she dumped him."

"Good," said Robbie, flat and firm. "Good for you."

The sun tipped behind the trees and took some heat with it. Neither of them moved.

"So it was junior year?" Robbie said slowly. Margaret let out a long, slow breath.

Robbie put his hat back on. "I remember I finally got up the nerve to ask you to come four-wheeling, and you said yes, but then you didn't show. Then I was sitting behind you in biology a couple days later, and everybody was talking shit about Parker scoring some girl in the woods behind school. I tried to talk to you, but you were gone. It was like you'd walked away." He cast a loose hand in front of him. "I thought it was me. I thought I'd done something."

"The south hill," Margaret said. "Not the woods."

He touched his chest. "Well anyway, Trina and me figured out what must have happened. There were rumors. It makes me pretty sad, thinking about it."

"They're pulling down those trees. Bulldozed the whole hill. To make room for the new baseball field. For the new wires."

"I'm glad," Robbie said.

Margaret put her cup down on the sidewalk. "I want to go back inside now, Robbie."

He didn't say another word. He got in his truck. Margaret didn't see him go; he was in the black edges of the cartoon circle closing around her. *That's all, folks.* She went inside, finished her shift, then drove home and didn't talk to anybody for two whole days. Julie called. Robbie called. She didn't pick up. She was worried if she opened her mouth she would howl or wail or speak in tongues like a backcountry preacher and wouldn't be able to stop until she screamed so hard her throat bled and she was cut open from the inside, so she just took sick leave and stayed home, mute and motionless.

***

At the end of the second day, Margaret emailed Robbie and told him she'd do whatever he wanted. In bed. She wouldn't tell Trina. He could pick her up after work, and they could go out to the cabin, if he still wanted. Nobody had ever asked her to do those sex things before. She was thirty-three and didn't know how to be anybody's partner, but she figured if she was going to give this a whirl, Robbie made the most sense to try it with. And she could type, not speak, which made it easier. She clicked and swiped and imagined the words traveling on wires Robbie had hung with his own hands between the county's spindly, pocked telephone poles. She said yes. To the butt stuff, to everything in his list. If he still wanted.

***

Robbie replied and said he'd pick her up after work, and they could talk, just talk. He said he'd only been with a handful of women, one before marrying and a couple after, so Margaret didn't have to feel awkward about not being experienced. He wasn't either, not really.

"How come you want me to do that thing with my finger?" she asked him the next day. They were sitting in his truck at the Sonic.

Robbie's cheeks pinked above his beard. He had the beginnings of crow's feet, but his eyes were still pale and boyish. He shrugged. "Guess it just seems like it would feel good."

"Can't you ask Trina?"

"I've never been good at asking her for things. You don't have to do it if you don't want to." His phone buzzed on the seat next to him. He snatched it up and stilled it, then tucked it under his leg and drummed his fingers on the steering wheel.

Margaret sucked on her straw while Robbie hid his phone. The wife, she figured.

"I still will. It's not *that* freaky."

"Can we not do this at the cabin, though?" he asked. "Or your place? It's a little—it makes me nervous, is all. If it goes wrong . . . if I screw it up, I don't want there to be any awkwardness, like, left over, in your bedroom. Or mine."

Margaret looked around. "Well, I don't know if I'll feel very sexy squished up here in your truck."

"What about a hotel? We could meet there. I've, uh, I've done that before," he said. "Then we've both got a way out if we need one."

Margaret said she thought that sounded like a fine idea, and they settled on the following Thursday to meet at the Holiday Inn three miles from GameStop.

***

Early the next week, Margaret called her sister and asked if she could borrow her snakeskin stilettos. Julie's voice fizzed and echoed in Margaret's ear.

"Are you going to a costume party?" she asked, laughing.

"Sort of." She wasn't going to say anything about Robbie. Not a word. "Can I get them Thursday?"

"I guess. Don't scuff them, though. They cost a lot."

"I'm not even going to wear them outside. I might not need them."

"OK, um, but come by before six."

Margaret and Robbie spent the next few days practicing kissing each other on their lunch breaks. Their first time he parked behind the GameStop, facing into the scraggly bank of trees behind the strip mall, where nobody could see.

"I want to get used to you," Margaret said.

She leaned forward and nuzzled him. She skritched her fingers in his beard and smelled him. His hair reeked of pine. Robbie leaned back against the driver's door. She pecked him on the lips, a soft flash of wetness. Then she put her knees on his seat and gripped the headrest to steady herself. Her head was above his, and she looked down at him. She felt large and electric. She kissed Robbie with tongue and found he tasted like cloves, with a mossy, metallic aftertaste that reminded her of river rocks.

Margaret let go of the headrest and gripped his shoulders, rubbed his thigh. No fear rose in her, nor did her body fill with lead. Instead she felt tingly and lithe, and the backs of her knees got sweaty. Robbie grabbed her elbow and eased her back for a breather. He put a cool hand under her shirt, resting it on her belly. She could tell he was surprised at how adept she was at making out.

"I've *dated*," she said. "Not a lot. But still." She wiped her mouth and sat back in her seat. "I'm not a nun."

Robbie exhaled and tucked his chin. "OK then!" he said, beaming.

Margaret gathered up her purse and climbed out of the truck. She glanced back and said, "I like kissing," and they both cracked up laughing.

***

On Thursday, Margaret tried to act extra normal at work. She left around five and drove to Julie's house for the stilettos. She still wasn't sure she would wear them, but she had amassed a small bag of accessories, and she wanted to be prepared.

Gathering a sex bag was furtive business. She couldn't bring herself to buy condoms in Bentley, so she had driven to a Walgreen's almost all the way in Lexington. She also had massage oil, three bras, a bottle of wine, and almost all her toiletries. She put everything in her navy gym duffel and kept checking the back office to make sure nobody snooped inside it.

The whole of Richland Skyway popped raw colors at her as she pulled out of work and drove to her sister's house. Bright burger joints, stark blue gas station lettering. She caught every light, and at each one she eyed the red bulbs inside their yellow metal housings. She stared at telephone poles and followed their wires into the distance. Her whole field of vision was cut up with lines. People forgot to see them; they were so common they disappeared.

When she pulled up to Julie's house, a strange, hulking SUV with chrome wheels was sitting out front. Maybe one of the lawyers from work, or maybe Uncle Jack had traded in his sports coupe. Instead of marching in as usual, she rang the doorbell.

Julie answered the front door with Parker Hackett's hand under her tit.

"Hey, come on in," her sister said, giggling at Parker.

"Hey, Peg," said Parker from behind Julie. His face was blank.

"Uh," Margaret said. The small of her back iced over.

"Ssshh!" Julie said, and slapped his chest. "You know she hates that."

Parker's eyes were dark and small. His hair was a plain, solid shield of chestnut. He wore khakis and a button-down. He looked healthy and scrubbed. Standardized. They hadn't seen each other since a tense family Christmas at her parents' place in Florida three years ago. Margaret glared at him until his jaw muscles thickened into cords and he slid his thin hands off her sister.

"I'm gonna get a beer, babe." His voice was taut, higher pitched than she remembered.

Margaret didn't move.

Julie said, "Are you coming in?"

"Julie," she said. "What the fuck."

Her sister raised a hand. She touched her face, and her bracelet caught the light like it always did. "Oh. I've been meaning to tell you. I don't know, Margaret. It just happened."

"When?"

"Last month? Jack and I aren't working out. The age difference . . . And the girls love having Parker here." She tilted her head, touched her chest. "He's their *dad*."

"Julie." She shut her eyes tight. "Just please shut the fuck up."

"All right," said Julie. She backed away and reached for a long pink shoebox on the carpeted stairs behind her. "God."

Margaret clenched her fists, but she couldn't hold them tight. Parker standing there in the door with his hands all over Julie. The image weakened Margaret's triceps, and her arms flopped to her sides. She wished everyone would understand: you can't throw punches at people like Parker Hackett. It's not even worth trying. Your body slackens, and it stays that way.

"I know you don't like him," said Julie, "but at least be happy for me." She held the shoebox out, then pulled it back slightly. "Or maybe you do like Parker. Still. Is that it?" Her tone was low and sweet. She spoke the same way she talked about the poor kids in her daughters' class, the ones who ate free lunches and rode the rural route bus. The same tender pity.

Margaret's temples throbbed. Her skin felt grimy and slick.

"So you're a little jealous. So what, honey? You'll find somebody. Just, you know, don't make things our fault."

Julie shifted her hips, and Margaret clenched her teeth.

"Hey, why don't you call whatshisface when you get home from your shoe thing?" She reached out to stroke Margaret's hair. "From the reunion? Robbie. I bet he likes you."

Margaret batted away her sister's hand.

"OK," Julie said, "God. Never mind."

Lots of people in high school had thought Peg had a crush on Parker. Peg, *Margaret*, had not. But there was no way to protest, to say no without sounding hollow and weak. Nobody would believe her. Not even her sister. On the front step in her high shoes, Julie towered a foot above her.

"How can you let a man like that around your *daughters*?" she asked.

Julie's face tensed. Her smile went hard. Her pupils flickered with a quick, tiny light, but then the light went away, and she was still. Her teeth looked like dull plastic.

"I don't know what you mean," she said.

"Julie," said Margaret. "How."

"Enough." Julie held up a finger. "You don't have anything to say." She huffed and shook her head. "Did somebody tell you something at the reunion? You don't know." Julie looked down at Margaret's chest. "You've never."

The girls giggled inside the house, and the sound lilted toward them.

Parker leaned into the hallway and called, "Hey, get in here, momma. Bring ol' Peg with you."

Both women's bodies tightened, as if they were a pair of maids snapping sheets under a clothesline, as if they were facing each other and folding them, together.

Julie was still holding the box. "Do you want the shoes or not?"

Margaret threw up her hands and marched back to her car. She flung open the driver's door and faced the house. Hot metal rose up from her gut. This was the part that scared her—when the hidden thing inside tried to get out but couldn't take form. Her lungs burned, and she couldn't latch onto words.

Then, with all her might, Margaret tipped up onto her toes and bellowed the first thing that came to her.

"Goddamn it," she thundered. "You need to talk to TRINA BAGSHOT!"

Then she flopped into the car and spun out of the driveway, white-knuckling the wheel.

***

On the way to the Holiday Inn Express, Margaret thought about throwing every last pair of her sister's heels into the road and driving over them a billion times. She thought about checking into a different hotel and scrubbing every inch of her skin under a hot, white-tiled shower over and over to get herself clean. She thought about fucking Robbie Barnwell in a thousand different positions and showing everybody what she was made of. She thought about going back to Knoxville and sending Trina a handwritten letter in the mail. As far as she could tell, Trina was the only human being in all of this mess.

Everything felt ruined. She needed another two days of silence to crush things back down inside herself again, but nobody was going to give her that kind of time. She had a date. She was supposed to do things with Robbie, who had kept silent with her. And she still wanted him, kind of, even now.

"Can I just lay down?" she asked. Robbie had texted her the room number, and somehow she had got herself to the door.

He stepped back for her to enter. His movements were smooth, as if his center of gravity had shifted downward since she'd last seen him. "You look pale," he said. "Are you sick?"

Margaret walked inside. The room was decorated in modern colors, spare and spotless. The silver bedspread had a grid of thin black stripes crisscrossing it.

"Julie's been seeing Parker," she said.

"Oh," said Robbie. "Shit."

She stared at the bedspread. "Can I just lay down? Robbie, can I do that?" She sat on the edge of the bed and ran her hand along a white pillow. It felt smooth and cool. She had forgotten her sex bag, her navy gym duffel stuffed with supplies. Her body started to shake.

Robbie sat on the other side of the bed. His shirt pocket lit up and buzzed, but he ignored it. The glow from his phone swelled through the thin blue cotton and illuminated his chest.

"Margaret," he said, "you can do whatever you want. You don't have to do a thing in the world."

Margaret stood. She put her hands under the sheets, pushed into their coolness up to her elbows, and drew them back. She climbed in, shoes and all, and pulled the covers over her face. She tried to stop shivering. Robbie didn't touch her, but he inched a little closer. She felt the bed sink as he lay down. The mattress warmed with his body heat, and his phone buzzed again.

"I'm sorry we're not doing this how I said we would," she said finally.

"We'll get around to it," said Robbie.

The blankets muffled her voice. "I'm sorry I didn't talk to you more in school or go to prom with you or whatever."

"I didn't ask you to prom," Robbie said.

"Yeah," she said. She closed her eyes. The covers pushed down on her.

"It isn't even your fault," she said. Her breath heated the sheets. "I'm sorry you can't have what you want. I'm sorry Trina doesn't do butt stuff with you or love you enough or whatever. I like Trina, but she's a dumbass for that. I wanted you to have a nice time. I'm just sorry, Robbie."

Robbie Barnwell, whom Margaret had known all her life, didn't respond. She felt him stretch out next to her on top of the grid-lined bedspread. His arm flopped onto the pillow above her, but otherwise he kept a foot of clean bedclothes between them. After a while, he began to breathe in an even rasp that matched the swish of traffic on the highway outside, and every few minutes, his phone buzzed and lighted. Its whirring traveled into the mattress. Margaret could feel Trina's vibrations in her spine.

They stayed in bed together for a long time. When the sun had set outside, Margaret pulled the shroud of covers off her face. She gasped cool air and turned to Robbie's shadowy, still body beside her. His mouth was open, lips half-pursed. He still smelled like pine, but there was a musty undertone to the scent now. Robbie's phone peeked askew from his breast pocket, its blue notification light blinking every few seconds. The flash reminded her of a lighthouse.

Margaret listened to Robbie's snoring, smelled his pine-musty breath for a few more minutes; then she slipped out from under the warm linens. She stood and rubbed her hands slowly along her sides to smooth her rumpled clothes.

Never mind. Never mind any of it, she thought, and she took herself home in the dark.

PARKWAY

We find bodies all the time. Lots of folks come up here to die or kill or get killed. My first one came in the summer. We were up Back Branch, near the Virginia border, where the tree line thickens above the bald. It was me and Coralis, who trained me when I started with the park service. Coralis taught me pretty much my whole job, and the only part I've ever questioned is whether he taught me how to deal with the living and the dead the right way around.

That first time, Coralis and me were heading from Back Branch to Sugar Knob. This was back in '93, my first month on the job, before I got my own vehicle. I was one of the only woman rangers in the whole state then. We were heading north, coming out of an early morning fog, and we saw a flash off to the right, like a gleam off somebody's smile in those old toothpaste commercials. We thought that was strange with it so gray and misty, so we checked it out.

Coralis pulled over in the grass near a mile marker—the old stones, white and square, the ones you see all along the whole length of the parkway. When tourists first see them, they pull over to take pictures, touch the hand-carved numbers, but after a while, they stop caring and ignore them. Those markers look to me like little headstones, so I think people get creeped out after too many.

We hopped out of the truck, looked down the bank, and Coralis pointed into the woods.

"I see a wheel," he said.

We went down a few more feet, and we found this little old red Gremlin tucked down into the trees, like somebody hid it on purpose. She was in there.

Through the rear windshield, we saw her long hair lying across the backseat, her head tilted at an unnatural angle. Her face was so white, I thought maybe she was sleeping. I kept inching toward the car; I guess part of me wanted to wake her up, whisper to her or stroke her hair to raise her.

Coralis gripped my shoulder to hold me back and said, "Call it in, Priscilla."

That might be the only time he ever touched me or used my real name. His voice had a cold rattle in it, and the words shook in his throat. My voice shook, too, when I radioed the ranger station.

I came back and stood next to Coralis, who clenched his teeth for a long time. Finally he said, "We should stay with her. Don't let's leave her alone, Pea. Not till they get here."

So we sat on the bank looking at her hair through that back windshield. State police arrived a while later, and homicide detectives and all. I stood out of the way when Coralis told me to let him handle it. Me being a woman and a rookie, I think he was worried I'd faint. I kept staring at the Gremlin while the cops took pictures, taped off a line, and the morning warmed itself.

A few hours later, as the coroner packed her away, Coralis said I'd have to get used to finding corpses now and then.

"Once a year," he said, "maybe twice. Mostly cliff jumpers and accidents, mostly intact, but sometimes only parts." He nodded at the body bag. "Sometimes frightful whole ones like her."

I crossed my arms and stifled a sob. I was real young then, young-minded, I mean, and I had never thought I'd have to do this kind of work. I just wanted to be in the woods.

"Now comes the paperwork," Coralis said. His face wasn't stern like usual, and the deep lines around his eyes held less shadow. He didn't smile exactly, but I could tell he was glad to have found her. "Come on, I'll show you."

On the way back to the ranger station, Coralis told me a bunch of stuff.

"This job is boring as hell most of the time," he said. Then he went on about how I'd spend less time than I wanted outside, and instead I'd just drive forever along the tops of mountains. I'd have to deal with things I couldn't quantify, and some of the male rangers might hassle me, but mostly I'd get to work in my own way.

"In the end," he said, "it's a fair deal, as long as you take care of the worst things."

"Like her," I said, thumbing back to the scene behind us.

Coralis nodded. "Nobody wants to see that on vacation. You have to look at it for them."

We rode in silence for a while, both of us watching the mountains, until the forest closed in and made a tunnel of green.

"I guess it makes sense to dump a body up here," I said.

Coralis didn't say anything until the thick canopy opened onto a valley view.

"People use parks for selfish reasons," he said.

He pulled into a scenic overlook and cut off his truck. Slowly, he let go of the steering wheel and cast his hands toward the narrow valley below us. "Four hundred miles of parkway through some of the prettiest country there is, and everybody brings their shit." He leaned forward and shook his head. "There's more murders, starved dogs, more toddlers slipping off cliffs, more sadness than anybody knows." He glanced at me, then at the road behind us, and shrugged. "We clean it up. Then maybe we give a tour, hand out some brochures. Almost nobody knows where they're going. Maintain order, even when there isn't any. That's all."

It was the longest conversation he and I ever had.

We never did figure out what lit up, what made the flash we saw before we found her. The Gremlin had a rusty old bumper; no chrome, so that couldn't have been it. Maybe a bird flew past carrying something shiny, or the light was playing tricks, or maybe we were just supposed to find her.

The coroner said the girl had been there about three days, dying slow from deep wounds in her chest and guts. I only saw her face, white and clean, never any of the blood, which I was glad of.

Turned out it was her cousin who had killed her. They caught him pretty quick, and we had to go to the trial a few months later. I was working my own routes and had my own truck by then, but the morning he was called to testify, Coralis picked me up early and we went to the courthouse together. He wore a suit that looked a hundred years old. I climbed in his truck and saw him all pleated and grim in his charcoal three-piece straight out of some museum painting, and I laughed.

"Why're you wearing that getup?" I asked him. "Coulda just worn your uniform."

Coralis gripped the gear shift and stared straight ahead.

On the stand, Coralis explained to the jury about finding her. I sat in the back of the courtroom and kept still. Coralis talked in a flat one-two, methodical, looking down at his veiny hands, about how we came upon her, how we stayed with her. The victim's family was up front with their backs to me. They leaned on each other, and I watched the light hitting them while their shoulders shook from crying. That girl seemed real close and fresh to me while Coralis talked. I studied her family a good while, but none of them had hair like hers.

***

I remember every body I've found the same as I remember that girl. I remember mostly how soft they always look, especially the accidents, if you can see their faces. Sometimes if they've been dead a while, the bugs have got to them, or they've been cut by a windshield or somebody's slashed them up. Even then, it's little things that make me go tender. Like the way a body's feet are laid out. A lot of people when they die turn their feet inward, just like a baby does when he's napping deep. Over the years, after what I've found, I believe we all get warm before we go. We sink down into some warm place like we did in our cribs when we were little.

Most bodies I found had special marks, or little objects that surprised me. Five years ago, right after my youngest niece was born, I was on overnight south of Asheville, moving a fawn's body off the road where she'd been hit by a car. I had my headlights trained on myself while I picked up the fresh carcass. She was still warm, even in the December chill, her body a velvety sack of limbs. As I stood to carry her off, I noticed the hand-painted billboard for the quilting museum about twenty yards ahead. It came to me that I should look behind it.

Bodies have beacons, I think. They want to get found.

I laid the fawn in my truck bed, took off my gloves, and went to him. He was leaned up against the back of the old quilting museum sign, staring glassy into the forest. No more than twenty years old, small and delicate, dead only a few hours from what looked like an overdose. A thin line of drool sparkled like a glass needle from the corner of his mouth. He had this little purse, a bag he carried, and for whatever reason he was still holding it when I found him. The bag had cats on it made out of white sequins, with little black whisker threads sewn in lines around the faces. It looked homemade, with perfect, tight stitches. There was something about him hanging on to that purse; I thought my heart might split.

I squatted down, and how it was, was I talked to him. I wanted him to know he wasn't alone. I told him who I was, what I did; I talked about the fawn and how I'd come to be there. I told him how the grass looked around him in the dark, inky and cool.

People think it's peaceful here, I said, but it's not. I put one hand in the grass to steady myself. Nobody should come up here if they can help it. But I could see him, I said. He was found. I rubbed my throat to slow my breath. I'm here, I said.

I walked into the road and reached for the radio on my shoulder. Stood in the middle of the silent blacktop and called parkway dispatch and the sheriff. Then I came back and sat down. Authorities'll be along, I told him, and you'll be home soon, with your family or whoever's waiting on you.

I stared at the road; he looked into the forest. We both settled into the stillness. He was slumped sideways, one shoulder up higher than the other. His skin wasn't scary like it could have been. Every part of him, even his clothes, was soft purple in the moonlight, like lavender paper. State bureau never did figure out who he was.

***

Coralis's half sister Rita works at the casino in Cherokee; I see her sometimes when I take my nieces to their dance competitions. I went to find her and play some slots the day after I heard Coralis was dead. Rita told me I was the only person he'd ever agreed to train or allowed to ride with him.

Rita's mom, Coralis's stepmother, was EBCI, so he went to the tribal school part of every year. Rita said when they were kids, Coralis would always get in trouble at recess.

"He'd never come in," she said. "The teachers would have to go find him. He'd be over at the creek, catching salamanders or watching elk. He never changed. Hardly ever talked, even back then."

I said that must have been rough, not having your big brother talk to you. Rita just shrugged. Then she gave me a drink voucher and said, "Least he figured out the right line of work for himself."

She tapped a long fingernail on her empty drink tray. "Just like you, Miss Pea."

***

Coralis died from a heart attack. He was on duty, five days before he hit forty years of service, and two months before I hit twenty years myself. He sat down in front of his truck at the top of Herman Falls and passed on alone. If he made a noise, no one heard him over the white water rushing into the gorge. I felt bad for not being the one who found him, even though we didn't work the same counties anymore. He never talked to the other rangers much, and he'd gotten even quieter in recent years. The last time I saw him, he was sulking around the rangers' station. I made small talk at his mumbles, then he made like he wanted to hand me an article on that big garbage patch in the Pacific. He didn't look at me, just gripped the paper like he couldn't let me have it. Then he walked off with it still in his fist.

I felt bad, too, that I hardly knew his people. I met his wife a few times before they divorced, and I see Rita when I go to Cherokee, but that's all. Then again, I'm not sure Coralis saw his people himself much. None of his grandkids came to the funeral. We delayed the ceremony for them, but then Pastor said they'd got the times confused and hadn't even left Knoxville, so we carried on with the celebration of life with a lot of empty chairs.

Everybody talked to me after the service longer than they talked to Rita. Lots of people offered me condolences.

Suzanne, who works dispatch up at the ranger station, patted my hand and said, "I'm so sorry, Pea. I know you two were best friends."

Being Coralis's best friend was news to me.

After the funeral, I decided I'd better take early retirement and find another job soon, while my family still knows my name. My wife, Danielle, told me I'm not allowed to talk about the parkway anymore. Coralis dying made me gloomier than ever. Even without the bodies, I'm not up to the job. Used to be we could live off what the park service paid, but they keep cutting benefits, and there's more territory now since the state parks have started to close, and fewer rangers to cover it, and nobody to keep our trucks running. Last winter I had to buy my own tires, and I go out for longer and longer days.

Danielle doesn't want to hear it.

"Don't talk about it in the house," she says. "It puts a blanket over everything."

***

I didn't quit until the last body. The teacher, six weeks ago. I found him when I was closing the main gates up at Old Balsam. We got hit with a March blizzard, always the worst, so we were scrambling to clear traffic and shut access ramps before anybody got trapped.

It was snowing hard, and the evergreens around me were catching white thick and fast. There was no beacon or pretty flash like the others. No ease or calm. I didn't think there was a body waiting. Instead I felt cold slip under my collar, felt anger all around me. I clunked the pin into the entrance gate and I stood there in the snow.

I was supposed to wait, so I did.

It didn't take long to see him. It was like my eyes were dragged, like they had to pull to the left and look to the hemlocks. My eyes couldn't *not* look. And I got that feeling in my stomach similar to what I got all those other times I found a body, but this time it felt worse, as bad as anything. This time harder and darker. Snow coming down all around me heavy and mean, my truck engine humming twenty feet behind, churning warmth too far to reach. My eyes pulled left, then up and along the hillside at the tree line. It felt like the moment before somebody fires a bullet, except the gun never goes off. As tense as that.

At first I thought some coyotes had got a big kill, maybe a calf from a nearby farm. Most of the blood had been snowed over already, in that short time, even though he'd just done it. I got there soon after, real soon. It looked to me like meat hanging for a butcher.

My knees bent. I wanted to run, jump in the truck. But this job moves muscles for you, so even though I wanted to crouch and hide and run, the whole time thinking somebody's behind me, or in front, or all over, instead I stood still and reached inside my jacket to call it in and follow procedure. I can't help but do what I'm supposed to.

The snow eased up for a few seconds, and everything came clear. I saw his legs. His legs and back, blood everywhere. It looks so lonely, so human, the shape of a person's legs hanging down. Something broke in me, and I started talking, real high pitched, saying nothing, rattling and whining like I did when I was little and my daddy would get drunk and belt me. I made that same baby gibber talk; it flowed out of me into my radio, into the cold.

His legs were the only part of himself he hadn't cut up. Everything else he'd carved and splayed. The examiner's report, when I read it a few days later, said he removed his clothes slow and careful, climbed up, tied a noose, and sat in those thick hemlock boughs doing things to himself until he fainted from the pain and dropped from his own gallows.

I didn't know any of this then, of course. The homicide detective had to tell me three times before I'd believe her, and I still wanted to read the report later on. In the moment, I figured murder. I figured whatever did that was still around, and maybe I was scared it wasn't even a person or animal that had done it, but another thing entirely. I don't know what else I thought it could have been, but I was alone out there with it.

The branches swung him a little, and his body turned toward me. His face looked torn and wrong, and his guts were hanging out.

Fire finally welled in my legs, and I spun and scrambled. I fumbled into the truck and locked the doors, breathing *whoosh-whoosh* like a woman giving birth. All I thought was get out, get out, go, but it seemed like whatever had brought that body was everywhere, and I couldn't escape.

I radioed again, giving details as best I could. Suzanne was on dispatch that day, and she could barely recognize my voice.

I shut my eyes tight as they'd go, but then I was afraid of what might see me while I wasn't looking. So I opened my eyes and looked straight ahead. The snow fell like a sheet. I yanked the truck into gear and drove in tight circles in the gravel turnaround beside the gate, just so I could be moving. If something jumped down or came for me, I could gun the accelerator and drive off. I did that for an hour, circling, keeping the body just on the edge of view, waiting for the thud of flesh or beast against my door, until backup got there and I didn't have to be alone with him anymore. I wouldn't get out of my truck until four deputies and a fire truck arrived.

***

Danielle heard about the teacher on the news before I got home. It was a big story, and the snowstorm kept me at the scene and the police station for a whole day. By the time I walked in the back door, she had worried herself into one of her headaches.

I stood on the wet floor mat, and the first words out of my mouth, my first words to my wife were, "Who goes to that much trouble?"

I still had my coat on, and the linoleum was covered in slush I'd tracked in. I unlaced my boots, kicked them off, and stood in my sock feet. The television in the living room was bouncing blue light off the kitchen countertops.

"Pea," Danielle said, "why in the world don't you just leave it?"

She reached out and tugged at my heavy coat sleeves, one at a time, back and forth. It rocked me off balance, and I tottered like a child.

"We got options," she said. "We could go someplace warm together."

"You think?" I leaned close to her and whispered, "You think all this death wouldn't follow me?"

Danielle tugged at me again, and I felt my throat tighten around a sob. Then she backed away and got herself some water and more headache pills, and I undressed alone in the kitchen.

***

They put me on the standard mandatory leave after the teacher. After every found body, a ranger has to stay off the parkway for a week or two, depending on how bad the situation is. The regional deputy director took one look at me and said I had to take a month. He told me to eat and take care of myself, to let Danielle cook me something nice.

I had a few nightmares. In my dreams, the teacher's body would jump down from the tree and hurl itself at me, guts cut open, screaming for me through mutilated cheeks, beating my windshield with his bloody hands. Those nights were bad, but I got bored during the day, so I finally went to the ranger station and asked for desk duty. Suzanne gave me a bunch of filing to do. I went through old personnel records, purchase orders, that kind of thing. Most of it we destroyed. Suzanne said they keep everything on the computer now, so we shredded piles of National Park Service history.

They also required me to get counseling at a psych practice in West Asheville. It looked hippie-dippie, stuck in some creaky-floored Victorian house with pale green walls and wind chimes on the porch. I had to do three sessions, and I had to talk about the bodies.

The first session, the therapist made me do a visualization exercise to calm myself after the Traumatic Event. That's what he called it.

"Just pay attention to your breathing," the therapist told me. "Find a place where you're completely comfortable."

I stretched out on the long tweed couch in his office, closed my eyes, and pictured my brother-in-law's place down on the coast.

I lay on his itchy sofa and felt the air passing in and out of my chest, the tweedy fabric digging little needles into my back through my cotton shirt. I crossed my arms over myself between my breasts and thought about the flatness of the coast, the warmth. I love my brother-in-law's driveway, how long and open it is—treeless and sandy hot. I kept staring down that driveway until my toes curled, and I almost could see the ocean. The therapist's sofa started to smell beach-musty instead of mold-musty, and I eased into a warm place. I could see what was coming. The emptiness in front of me was clear and straight, free of switchbacks, no fog. I felt Danielle beside me, the quiet between us easy and soft, like it used to be, not tense like it had been lately. Afterward I figured maybe the therapist knew what he was doing.

In my last session, the therapist got all whispery and asked if I ever read Dante or if I knew about the boatman on the Styx. I said sure, but I didn't understand the connection, except sometimes after it rains, the asphalt on the parkway can look black and winding like a river. And anyway, after what the teacher had done to himself, I didn't want to carry his body or help him, not like I helped those other people I found.

***

When my mandatory leave was over, I went on rotation for a couple of days. I worried maybe I'd have the shakes or see shadows.

I spent the first day at Waterrock watching Harleys thrum past and shake the spring buds. It seemed like there were thousands more visitors than usual, all louder than before. I watched tourists stop at the overlook and take pictures. Everyone moved strangely, spoke in echoes, as if their bodies were hollow.

I spent the second day in the elk trail lot. I sat on my bumper with my arms crossed over the park patches on my chest. I tried to talk to folks, but I had cottonmouth. Somebody asked me for directions to a waterfall, and I couldn't remember which milestone to send them to. So I climbed in the truck and watched everybody from there. Nothing connected. No flow or rhythm to the traffic, no breeze whirling a pattern in the leaves.

The parkway had this gloss on it, like a plastic apple I couldn't eat. I thought about Coralis all alone at Herman Falls, and I went home finished. There's going to be more bodies like the teacher, and I don't want that job.

I went up to the ranger station this morning to put in my separation papers and talk to Suzanne one last time. Our station sits above five thousand feet, in among the spines of evergreens stripped bare by invasive adelgids. The station is the last place in three states to see any leaves in spring, and those skeletons poke out from the maples and poplars all year round. I used to love to end my shifts up there, with the hushed Blue Ridge undulating in every direction and birds calling down in lonesome coos.

This morning the ranger station seemed like the worst place I could be. I didn't want to be among dead trees or watch the blue valleys. I don't want to be above all that, looking down into it.

Suzanne seemed real sorry about it when I told her I was leaving, but I didn't let her pat my hand this time. I held my arm up to keep her off me and told her me and Danielle were moving to the coast. That'll be news to Danielle, but I'm pretty sure she'll go along with the idea.

Milestones and bodies. These ridgelines can't hold them anymore. Coralis was right about people using parks for selfish reasons. We empty sorrow and trash out of ourselves into them, and now everything is harrowing up and spilling out from the boundary. I have to look away.

TWITCHELL

For the first half of Margie Pifer's pottery lecture at the Arts Council picnic, Iva Jo Hocutt thought the Russian girl was asking for a tampon.

"What?" Iva Jo whispered. "No. I don't know." She dodged the Russian girl's mortified stare for the fifth time; Iva didn't want Margie Pifer to think she wasn't listening.

The Russian girl was shaking her head and ignoring everyone but Iva Jo. On the little stage at the front of the white rental tent, Margie Pifer was lecturing about "the mountain craft tradition." Iva Jo sat in the second row of folding chairs, in the very last seat. She was bored and hot and thirsty, and her body felt to her today like a series of lumps. She wore a loose pair of linen capri pants and a gray Arts Council T-shirt. Iva stuck her leg out a few inches, just beyond the shade of the tent. The sun cast a bright, hot shard of July onto her freckled shin.

The tent was next to the soccer field, which was across the street from the elementary school where Iva Jo was the head office assistant. The whole complex occupied the left hand of the stippled body of Queensport, Tennessee, a valley town in the green Blue Ridge where Iva Jo spent her life. Houses dotted Queensport's seventeen capillary-thin streets, and Main was its spine. The Arts Council picnic was held every summer in this northwestern outskirt; the buzzing tents and booths looked from above, from atop the mountains, like colorful beetles held in the town's palm.

The Russian girl was perched alone on a bench a few yards from the tent, directly in Iva's line of sight. The bench occupied a shadowy patch under two willows.

Margie Pifer held up a big, rustic, multicolored bowl. She was made almost entirely of angles, so the swooping arcs of the bowl's edges looked sloppy in her hands.

"Sanitary," the Russian girl hissed again, her smooth, pale cheeks blushing livid.

Iva Jo squinted.

"There is blood," the Russian girl mouthed. She bared her teeth. "You have sanitary?" Her *h* in the word "have" was wet and phlegmy.

The mention of blood shook some compassion from Iva Jo, and she wondered briefly what she could do to help, but she didn't have anything in her purse. Iva was forty-nine; she hadn't had a period in months.

Poor thing, thought Iva, remembering the embarrassments of teenage menstruation. A breeze thwopped the tent's taut roof and wafted across the crowd. She ran a ring finger under each of her eyes—blue, bright, her best feature, she always thought—to wipe the sweat pooling there and focused on Margie Pifer and her bowl. Knowing Margie, there might be a quiz later.

Finally the Russian girl pointed at Iva Jo's feet with a rude thrust. The girl's delicate, quivering finger compelled Iva to pick up a foot and look at her sandal.

She was bleeding all over herself.

Two scarlet rivulets were dribbling down Iva's thick calf. Her green capris were soaked almost black, her white plastic chair an abattoir. She had no cramps, had at this moment no sense of herself emptying out. Iva Jo felt nothing now except piercing alarm radiating across her scalp.

In the universal synchrony women find in such moments, Iva Jo and the Russian girl set about a tacit, determined series of looks, signals, movements. First, Iva looked up at the Russian girl in white horror and humiliation. The Russian girl snapped into dutiful action. She rooted around and found a crumpled paper tablecloth, recently blown hither from some other tent. The Russian girl snatched it up and signaled Iva with wide eyes. *I am coming.* Iva eyed back, *Thank you; please hurry.*

The Russian girl bent over, crouched low, and weaved her way around the tent poles separating them, trying not to be seen. When she got to Iva Jo, the Russian girl bobbed her head and gave more eyes to tell her to stand up, that she would cover her with the tablecloth. She put cold fingers on Iva's upper arm, which meant, *I will walk behind you; we are going inside the school, across there, to the bathroom, together.* Iva coded back with glances and tensed muscles that she needed her purse; someone would see the blood on her chair. The Russian girl shook her head and crouched even lower. *Leave them; they don't matter. Go.*

Iva Jo stood up slowly and made it four steps before she passed out cold.

***

When she got home from the hospital that night, she found that Margie Pifer had dropped off a casserole, a get-well card full of Bible verses, and the deformed bowl from her lecture.

Hank patted Iva Jo's shoulder as she eased herself onto the sofa. "You want a glass of tea or anything?" he said.

She asked for a Pepsi, and her phone buzzed. She picked up.

"I'm so sorry I missed your lecture," she said, stroking her stomach. "Mm-hm. Oh, now, don't worry, Margie. I feel fine."

She listened for a long minute. "Hank will, but I'm not hungry. I'm just sick of myself."

Iva listened again. Hank came in with a fizzing glass for Iva and a plate full of Margie's casserole. He turned on ESPN and muted it, then picked at the casserole.

"They cleaned me up, did an ultrasound. Said I need hormones. Mm-hm. No, they reckon that was the heat, made me pass out. But they don't know. I don't know."

She listened again, lips pursed. She fussed with the ties on her pajama bottoms. "No, Margie, I don't want to do that. Because it's *surgery*. Radical surgery."

Iva watched the baseball players on ESPN chew and spit and whomp their bats in the sparse grass. "Mm-hm. At least it's summer. Time off to figure things out. All right now. God bless you, too, honey."

She hung up, drank the Pepsi, and tried to forget about the rock of fear in her gut.

Iva went to bed early. She bled through the night, so much she had to get up three times. There was still no pain, only an elevated heart rate that roared in her ears like soft static. Finally she changed into a Depends she found in the guest bathroom, left over from an elderly aunt's visit. Iva lay in bed and longed for her mother. She wept. She prayed for a granny witch to appear in the backyard, thin and spooky like a haint, and spare her whatever health crisis was coming, to cast a spell or make her a magic poultice of roots.

Then nothing.

The next day it was like the blood had never happened. The thick, extra-long maxi pad Iva Jo stuck in her panties stayed dry apart from a few rusty streaks, and by supper time she was in a half-bright mood. She was patting out a couple of hamburgers when Hank came home from work and touched her on the shoulder.

"You all right today, girl?" he said, and sniffed the patty in her hands.

"You want more A.1. than that?"

Hank nodded and began to empty his pockets into a basket on top of the microwave. He ran his hands into the various hiding places of his long body, the folds of his work pants, his work shirt. There were pockets on every limb. He produced four pens, a thin-framed pair of glasses, then a wallet, two sets of keys, a tape measure, a handful of change. He patted his broad chest, rubbed his backside, and frowned. The lines on his tan cheeks were deep and spidery.

"I left my—" he said, and held up two fingers. "Gonna run back out to the truck."

Iva Jo washed her hands, gathered dressings for the burgers, and opened a can of beans into a red pot on the stove. Her kitchen was dark but tidy. Theirs was a splanch-style house, and the kitchen and living room were on the sunken end. Iva's kitchen windows were flush with the ground. When she looked out, she saw the world through the trunks of hedges.

On her way past the microwave, she peeked into the basket and checked Hank's pocket leftovers. She looked for stray bits of paper, business cards scribbled with private numbers. Realtors liked Hank. His inspections were always spot-on and filed fast, so he got sent to a lot of the country clubs and newer developments. Lady realtors flirted with Hank. Lady realtors, Iva had observed, all had wispy hair and even, snowy teeth.

Hank returned with a thick binder, two clipboards, and a dozen spray roses wrapped in supermarket cellophane.

"There now," he said, passing the flowers to Iva, whose palms were still pink and clammy from handling the ground beef. "You're gonna be just fine."

***

At church the following Sunday, Pastor Rob said a special prayer for Iva Jo, which she appreciated. Hank wasn't much for religion, so she carpooled with Margie most weeks.

The church was First Baptist—large, brick, and stalwart at the base of Queensport's spine.

"Lord, we've had so much cancer in our congregation," said Mrs. Pickering after the service.

Mrs. Pickering was ninety and diminishing. She got confused about things.

"Iva doesn't have cancer," Margie said.

They were in line for refreshments, inching down a long, white, crowded hallway stretching from the main church into its newly renovated hall. Margie was wearing a sleeveless dress covered in tiny zigzags that matched her spiky hair.

"I had it in both my breasts," Mrs. Pickering went on. She gripped her cane and leaned against the oak doorframe of the Sunday school hallway. "My sister, too. And my niece."

Iva Jo tried to be helpful. "Two of my cousins had it. One was cervical. And Hank's brother's in remission from liver cancer." They moved up a few steps in line as the low murmur of the congregation swelled, subsided, then swelled again around them. The rhythm of chatty crowds. "It touches near about everybody."

Mrs. Pickering nodded. "All the local families, all the ones been here a good while."

Margie rolled her eyes. "Here we go," she mouthed at Iva.

"Makes you wonder. I've been wondering." Mrs. Pickering shut her eyes tight, lifted her face to the fluorescent light above, and shook her head. "I've been wondering years."

"Well, it's not Twitchell, if that's where this is going again," said Margie. "I've told you, Missus P, that's the price we pay for having jobs. Industry."

"I never worked there," said Mrs. Pickering. "Did you?"

Iva didn't answer. Margie stared at her, but Iva kept her eyes on

Mrs. Pickering, whose thin blouse, which looked like a daffodil, rippled as the old woman exhaled.

"My husband did," the old woman said. "Died of lung cancer. Never smoked a day."

"But he had benefits," said Margie. "Y'all were better off than if we'd been a coal town."

Stewie Pifer, Margie's husband, was the director of planning at Twitchell Chemical, the biggest employer in the county. Margie defended the company even after they got in trouble for all those EPA violations, even after they dumped eighty thousand gallons of corrosive slurry into Jubal Creek and poisoned twenty farms downriver. No one in the county drank from their own wells anymore.

Queensport and Twitchell were not special. Similar plants, and similar spills, abounded in the region, hidden up old logging roads, behind bribes. There was some talk of groundwater testing, a few settlements paid out. A film crew from the university tried to make a documentary. Not much else.

"Oh, my, yes," said Mrs. Pickering. "Coal is another thing altogether."

"Tourism's just as important, though, Margie," said Iva Jo. "Tourism's the future."

"But Twitchell's the last one standing. We can't all be *kayaking* instructors. People have got to have real work."

"Iva, what exactly is the trouble?" said Mrs. Pickering. "Pastor Rob didn't tell us."

"They're still figuring that out," said Iva Jo.

"Menopause," said Margie. "It's just the menopause, is all she's got."

"Ah," said Mrs. Pickering. "Don't you fret, now." She patted Iva's hand. "The Change is just terrible, but in the end, praise Jesus, you're free."

"Why go through it?" said Margie. "Do like me and get the hysterectomy. Best thing I ever did. I've been telling her. Be done with the whole mess."

"I'm going to see Dr. Philip this week," Iva Jo said.

"Well," said Mrs. Pickering, "I didn't go that route. Either way, you ought to find yourself a lady doctor. A female."

"She'd have to go all the way into Knoxville then," said Margie.

"Don't let a man cut you up," said Mrs. Pickering. She shook her head, squinted again. "They always want to cut. Get yourself somebody who understands a bit better."

The line had slowly advanced, and someone handed Mrs. Pickering a plate of cookies and offered to find her a seat. She took her leave and squeezed Iva Jo's wrist. "You hang in there, honey. It's just like giving birth. Just breathe full and ride it out."

Margie bit her lip and watched Mrs. Pickering dodder off. She handed Iva a paper cup full of watery coffee and pulled her by the arm into the church hall. "She's forgetful. That's all."

"Oh, I don't mind."

Iva knew Margie and her friends talked about her. They counted her miscarriages for years and told each other Iva Jo Hocutt *puts on a brave face*, that Hank Hocutt was *a good man for sticking around*. She never told anyone it wasn't something she mourned. Every time she'd lost a baby, relief had washed over her, warm and keen. Hank had never pushed the subject. Iva felt, at least on that one score, at least sometimes, like the luckiest woman in town.

"I'm so fortunate; I know that."

"Amen," said Margie, and held Iva's fingers in her own.

They sat at a plastic folding table near a narrow window and drank their coffee.

"I should do something for that Russian girl," she said. "The one who helped me. She was from Blue Sunshine. I should drive out there."

Iva knew the Russian girl was Russian because on the day of the picnic she'd seen her get off the Blue Sunshine Camp bus and herd a bunch of little ones toward the "Arts 4 KIDZ!" exhibits. The children had bounded toward a face-painting table in a haphazard stream, and the Russian girl and her colleagues had sighed and wiped their foreheads and looked for shady places to be alone.

Blue Sunshine Camp employed tons of them, more than most. The girls—mostly Ukrainian, not Russian, but Iva Jo always forgot this—worked on temporary visas as counselors in the camps throughout Sylvan County. The camps' huts and hiking trails skirted the boundaries of the national park, and every year they brought in Eastern Europeans to work in the woods for room, board, and a pittance. Iva Jo could always pick Russians out from a crowd. They all had the same plump lips, the same severe ponytails, and a pale, quiet fear of being so far from home. Some of them must have come from steppes or other flat places, because they ogled the Blue Ridge with wide eyes. They pointed at each mountain and compared them, making the rough shapes of peaks in the air with their hands.

Every summer they came. Slowly Iva Jo and her neighbors had started to see Russian girls in the winter months, too, after all the tourists left, after leaf season. Immigrants.

"Oh, no," said Margie, pulling her hand back from Iva's. "Don't go getting involved with all that."

"All what?"

"That girl's going home in a month or two anyhow." Margie looked around and lowered her voice. "At least, she better be. Being pregnant and all."

Iva Jo leaned forward. "What? That tiny little thing who wrapped me up in a paper tablecloth? She barely looked eighteen."

Margie nodded. "They found out right after she got here. Andrew said the whole camp knows. They're pretty upset with her. They think she was . . . you know. Already carrying it when she came over." Margie's nephew Andrew ran a laundry service. He delivered to a lot of the camps and knew all the staff gossip.

"So?"

"So," said Margie. "If she's too far along at the end of the summer, she can't fly home."

Iva Jo shrugged, shook her head a little. And?

"*So*," said Margie. "If she can't fly back to Moscow or wherever, she'll have to stay. Have the baby here. Then she's got herself a little citizen. *You* know."

Iva didn't know.

Margie rolled her eyes. "An *anchor* baby."

Iva Jo thought about the Russian girl's wide eyes, those downy eyelashes, and how earnest she'd been about helping her to the bathroom.

"Oh, I don't think she'd pull a scam."

"You'd be surprised," said Margie. "A lot of them do it. Out of wedlock and everything."

"That's not a big deal nowadays."

"Iva." Margie frowned. "Sunshine is a *Christian* camp."

"But Russians," said Iva Jo. "They go to church, don't they? None of this sounds too terrible. Sounds to me like she's just in a little trouble."

Margie sniffed a concession. "At least she's not Mexican. I doubt one of them would have helped you."

Iva Jo didn't say anything.

"Mexicans don't even come to the Arts Fair," said Margie.

"Did you invite any?"

***

The following day, Iva Jo drove out to Blue Sunshine. Scam or no scam, she owed the Russian girl her thanks. She waited until five o'clock, though, after all the daytime staff, the locals, the *Christians*, had gone home for the night.

The camp was a scatter of lodges, cabins, and metal gazebos all hodgepodged around the fork of Pigeon and Jubal Creeks. Iva's jeep wagon crawled up the dirt road past Blue Sunshine's stack-stone gate.

She gripped the steering wheel with both hands and ducked her head to look at every cabin and shanty she passed, trying to figure out which one might be the Russians' barracks. A thin-shouldered girl with a foreign look about her walked across the road carrying a toothbrush and a towel. Iva Jo watched the girl disappear into a sad-looking brown lodge behind some trees. Splotches of dark moss dotted its sagging roof.

Iva Jo pulled over and got out. She looked at the brown building, then at the rustling creek. The woods here made a canopy that blocked out sound and sun. Iva knew if she kept walking east from this spot, eventually she'd hit a stand of laurel trees bordering her eldest cousin's property. It was the biggest patch of laurel she knew of anywhere, and though it was too late in the summer for them, she still pictured their white blooms snowing the forest floor.

She walked in the direction of the lodge, then stopped in the middle of the dirt road. Iva closed her eyes and tried to imagine being young and in trouble in some foreign place. She tried to imagine sleeping in a camp counselor's dormitory bed and chasing after other people's children all day while suffering from morning sickness and tender breasts and the lonesome terror of a first pregnancy. Iva wondered, *How did she even see me? What makes a frightened girl hold a strange woman's hand and cover her with paper?*

"Can I help you? Are you a parent?"

She turned, and a clean-cut teenage boy addressed her again. "Are you lost?"

"I'm looking for—" Iva's tongue stopped behind her teeth. She didn't know the Russian girl's name. She thought she had brown hair, but it might have been blond. She couldn't be sure, and asking identifying questions would mean embarrassing both herself and her savior.

"Never mind," Iva said to the boy. "I'll find it."

She walked back to the jeep, climbed in, and drove home.

***

"Now, Iva," said Dr. Philip. "I don't want you to worry."

"Over what?" Iva Jo was sitting on the exam table. Her short hair was all mussed up at the back; she could tell when she touched it. The curls felt soft and twizzled, like they did after a day at the beach.

"Over what happened," he said.

"What *did* happen?" Iva was dressed. Her exam was over, and the smock she'd been wearing sat in a heap beside her. "I still don't understand why I bled like that. Out of nowhere."

"That's what we're trying to determine," said Dr. Philip. "You don't have a polyp. In the meantime, we'll start you on hormone replacements to help with your symptoms. It can take a while to get your dosage right."

The lights in the exam room glowed on his buzz cut. His hair was silver, the skin under it pale and bumpy. *Your head could be the moon*, thought Iva.

He wrote something on her chart. "You'll need to come back and see me in two months."

"So this is normal?" As she spoke, she swung her feet like a little girl.

Dr. Philip rubbed the back of his neck.

"Hard to calibrate. You're the right age for menopause." He flipped up a stack of papers in her file, a worn manila folder with feathery, gray edges. "And you've never carried a child to term, so this is all"—he bobbed his head back and forth—"sort of normal."

"I don't want a hysterectomy." She shifted her legs, rustling the table's paper cover.

Dr. Philip frowned. "You might not need one," he said. "But they work like a charm for a lot of patients. We do them all the time."

"I don't want one."

"We'll just see what's best, Iva." He clicked his pen. "By the way, when was your last mammogram?"

"You told me I didn't need one until I turned fifty."

Dr. Philip clicked his pen again. "Oh. Well, let's get the jump on that for sure. Every woman"—he smiled—"is different."

***

Iva Jo drove home from Dr. Philip's office with a purse full of scrips. She drove past the CVS, past Kmart, and two other places where she could have got them filled. She drove past the gated entrance to the Twitchell plant and didn't look at it. She didn't look at its long, familiar drive or its white smokestacks that loomed above town and glowed at night. She drove right past it all, through the whole body of Queensport, without stopping.

Hank got home around six o'clock and ambled into the living room. Iva was leaned back in her squat blue recliner reading a pamphlet called *Perimenopause: Your FAQs*.

"He says I need tests. Wants to try me on some pills."

"Tests?" said Hank.

"Well, a mammogram. And some blood work."

"You want me to come with?"

Iva laughed. "Oh, I don't think they'd let you. All those boobies everywhere."

Hank smirked, leaned against the bookshelf opposite her, and began to say something. His shoulder brushed the ugly bowl Margie had given her the week before. It wobbled on its base, tipped forward, and crashed to the hardwood floor.

"Oh," said Iva Jo, reaching out. She fumbled out of her chair toward the shelves.

Hank put his hands to his face, round eyed and sorry looking.

"Oh, Hank!"

"Careful, don't cut yourself. Stay back."

"I'll never live it down," she said. "That was her best piece."

Hank crouched down as Iva Jo slumped in the wreckage. She picked up a large, jagged hunk of glazed crockery, and a tendril of crude rage began to hum and tingle inside her.

"I'll glue it back together," he said.

"No," said Iva Jo. Hank reached toward the hunk of bowl. She slapped his hand away. "Get off. Get the *fuck* off."

He reared back. Iva swept her hands across the floor to gather the bits together.

"The hell? You didn't even like the damn thing," he said. "Hell, half the time you don't even like *Margie*."

"That's not the point," she moaned, and ran her hands again into the breakage.

"You'll cut yourself. All the little pieces."

"Sshh," said Iva Jo.

"Let me get my trouble light."

Hank jogged into the hallway and scooted around in the closet. She listened to him rustling, then felt the vibrations of his booted feet pounding back toward her. He pulled the trouble light onto his head, adjusted the straps, and knelt beside her. He reached up and twisted the light on. Its halogen beam blazed across the floor, and each shattered piece glowed.

"Let me do it," he said, reaching out.

She slapped his hand away again, harder this time.

"Get the brush. And the dustpan."

Iva had never slapped Hank before. The sensation of hitting him rung deep in her bicep. She couldn't tell whether she liked doing it; she only knew she felt like hitting him again.

"Goddamn," said Hank, standing up. "You're worse than the girls at the office." He cut off the trouble light's beam. "Every woman I know is on the rag this week."

Heat seared up her neck and across her face. She tasted sweat on her lips.

"Shut up," she said through her teeth. "Even if we were, it wouldn't matter. But we're not. None of us."

"Well," Hank said, dusting off his hands and backing away. His voice deepened. "Means the same to me either way."

Stop it, she thought. *Stop. Stop.*

***

"Elena."

"Hm?"

"Elena," said Margie. "That's the girl's name, the one who helped you. I asked Andrew."

They were in a grim, dingy medical office on a rank day in August, waiting for her first-ever mammo. Margie had tagged along for support.

"Elena," said Iva Jo, adding music to the syllables. "That's nice."

"Andrew said the daddy works at the same camp. I think he's Russian, too." Margie's hair, normally so blond and carefully spiked, looked wilted. It was early and already humid outside.

"What's she doing now?" asked Iva.

"Andrew said she went home," said Margie.

"What, back to Russia? You mean she's gone?"

"That's what Andrew said."

"And the father?"

Margie shrugged.

Iva blinked. "But what will she do? About the baby?"

"Miz Hocutt?"

Both women popped their heads up, and Iva reached for her purse. "Can my friend come with me?"

The mammographer gripped a metal clipboard and smiled. She wore a loose bun, no makeup, medical scrubs, and clogs. "It's a pretty tight squeeze in there. Your friend can wait out here and meet you afterward. Why don't you come on back?"

The exam room was about twelve feet square and filthy. The

floor was strewn with thick black wires and boxes of medical and office supplies. In the center was a massive beige machine that looked like those robots in the movies—the ones that can turn into cars. Everything was coated in a thin, gray fur of dust.

The mammographer, who barely met her eyes the whole time, gave Iva Jo a paper vest and a few instructions. She asked some questions about medical history, date of birth, the usual. One of the questions was "Have you ever worked at Twitchell Chemical?"

Iva stammered a little, then said no. The mammographer ticked a box and turned to the door. "Undress from the waist up," she said. "I'll be back in a minute."

Iva took off her blouse and reached back to undo her bra. She stared at the metal blinds on the window and hoped nobody could see in. She pulled on the blue paper vest and laid her purse and clothes over a chair in the corner. The mammographer knocked gently and came in.

"I'm big," said Iva, holding herself under the vest. She nodded at the machine, and the paper scratched against her neck. "I don't think my girls'll fit in that thing."

The mammographer produced a dark glass plate the size of a sheet of paper. "You'll be fine," she said.

For the next few minutes, Iva Jo hunched and contorted and gripped the sides of the machine like an awkward dance partner while the technician nudged Iva's torso and squished her breasts between the glass plates. Friends had told her mammograms were painful, but Iva didn't feel much. It reminded her of the gropings she'd giggled through with high school lovers. The plates weren't even cold. Then it was over, and she put her clothes back on, and Margie took her out for a fancy brunch of shrimp grits and mimosas.

***

A week later Dr. Philip called while she was folding sheets and said there was a "spot" in her right breast, and she might need a biopsy.

"Might," said Iva Jo.

"Often it's nothing. Could just be a bad image."

"Is this anything to do with that awful period I had? The bleeding?"

"No," said Dr. Philip. "Well . . . I don't think so."

"Do I have cancer?"

"That's unlikely, but we're just going to check and see."

Dr. Philip said the Knoxville Breast Center would re-scan the spot. If it turned out to be a lump, they would do the biopsy. He said they were very nice at the Knoxville Breast Center, and after her appointment there, Dr. Philip would give her the news one way or the other.

"How much is all this going to cost?"

"Depends on what they find," said Dr. Philip. "But again, it's probably nothing."

Iva's neck began to sweat.

"When will I know?"

"It'll take a while to get you in for a referral. A few weeks."

"Can't you do it? Can't you check me?"

"I don't have the resources here," he said. "This is a small town, Iva."

"Well," she said.

"Iva," asked Dr. Philip, "did you ever work at Twitchell?"

The dryer buzzed in the background. She leaned against the laundry room door.

"Because if you did," he said, "they might pay for some of your treatment. There was a big case a while back. Class action. There's a settlement fund."

"I remember," said Iva.

"Well, that might help some."

They both breathed into their phones.

"All that poison," he said. "It's a real shame what they did over there."

"Hank's gonna flip out," she told Dr. Philip, who told her not to worry.

***

The dingy breast clinic sent her a CD of her mammogram images to take with her when she went to Knoxville. She was curious and tried to look at them, to see inside herself, but the files wouldn't open on her laptop. A few days after that, she got a terse, official letter in the mail notifying her she had "high density breast tissue." State law required them to tell her that unlike average women, her boobs were mostly boob tissue, not fat, which made them hard to see through, so legally they couldn't be held responsible for any faulty images or future errors in diagnosis.

"What in the world am I supposed to do with this?" Iva Jo asked Hank.

Hank frowned at the letter. "Frame it," he said. "Means you got real knockers."

Iva Jo laughed, and Hank put his arm around her.

"Maybe I'll give it to Margie," she said.

Then she and Hank sat down and cried and prayed for a while.

***

Hank drove Iva Jo to Knoxville on a Tuesday near the end of summer. They stopped for breakfast at a diner and ordered mushroom omelets and talked about what they would do if she had cancer.

"I'll be right there," said Hank. "The whole way."

Iva Jo stared at the abstract watercolor on the wall above their booth. It looked like a sea.

"I don't think I want to be friends with Margie anymore," she said.

Hank opened a vial of creamer and poured it into his coffee.

"And I don't think I want Dr. Philip to be my doctor anymore. I shouldn't have had to wait this long to get all this sorted out. Lady at church told me she got all her results inside a week. All her tests and everything. And you know he hasn't called me back once? Not once. I've been going to him six years."

Hank nodded, sipped his coffee.

"We'll do this however you want, Iva," he said. "But I don't think we'll have to." He pointed his coffee cup at her chest, moved it back and forth. "I think everything's all right in there," he said, and took another sip.

"That Russian girl went home. Margie waited until she was gone to tell me."

Hank raised his eyebrows and poked a fork into his omelet.

"I guess I shouldn't have told her we broke her bowl."

"It was your bowl," Hank said. "She gave it to you."

Iva picked up her soda, took a sip. "How many people do you know have cancer?"

Hank swallowed a bite of omelet and raised his eyes to the ceiling to count. He rattled off names under his breath. "A lot."

"You think it's Twitchell? Everybody I know from those days got something."

Hank cleared his throat. "Does it matter? It's too late now. That was thirty years ago."

Iva drew her shoulders back. "Well, I never would've . . . If I'd known. I might've had a baby, even."

"Honey," Hank said. "You can't blame it on that."

"Well, it's obvious, isn't it?" she said. "Whole town suffering, breasts coming off everywhere, your brother's liver, lost babies, and nobody talking about it. They should tell us. The state. Doctors. They should investigate."

"That plant's been there since before we were born, Iva," said Hank. "We'd know by now if it was anything dangerous."

"Well, Margie should have told me, anyway."

"About Twitchell?" said Hank. "You want her snooping around those old silos?"

"No, about the Russian girl. Elena. I'd have gone to see her. Helped her. Found out what she did about her baby."

"Eat up," said Hank, crinkling a paper napkin. "We've got to get across I-40." He looked out the window. "All that traffic. I don't know how people live like this."

***

The Knoxville Breast Center looked like a spa. They had a fountain out front and valet parking. Hank kept his hand in the small of Margie's back while she filled out paperwork at the check-in desk. The check-in nurse told them to wait, Iva would be called back, no men were allowed beyond the lobby.

They had sleek leather chairs in the waiting area. They had real coffee and fishing magazines. The lobby was full of husbands.

"Iva Hocutt?" a woman in lavender scrubs called.

They both stood.

"OK, honey," said Hank. His voice tightened. "I'll be right here."

Iva Jo grabbed his hand.

"We'll know, Iva girl," he said. "At the end of this, we'll know. That's the main thing."

Iva Jo nodded and kissed his cheek. Hank gripped Iva's arm so hard she thought it might leave a bruise. Then she followed the lavender nurse through a thick wooden door.

The nurse brought her to a changing room. The doors to each room were slatted mahogany. It looked like a fancy department store.

"Everything off from the waist up," she said, "then pick your color!" The nurse waved to a wall of shelves stacked neatly with folded scrub vests. Pink, blue, some with moons and stars. "Find one that fits, and just tie it in the front. You can put your things in a locker outside. No purses. Keep your locker key with you."

Iva followed instructions. She chose a royal blue vest, a small locker. She put her purse, her blouse, and her bra inside, then pulled the key out of its lock and stretched its spiral lanyard around her left wrist. Her breasts flopped and swung as she walked to the waiting area. They felt soft, full. She pushed her arms against them to hold them in place, feel their warmth.

She waited. A tall woman in a pencil skirt led her into a white corner room and gave her a 3-D mammogram. The 3-D machine was fancier and cleaner than the one she'd danced with at the dingy clinic.

"We might let you go after this," said the 3-D woman. "Or they might call you back. Depends on what we find."

Iva waited. They called her back.

Ultrasound. A sage room. Warm and quiet. The sonographer wore pink scrubs and had a name tag. Mei. Thin face, a perfect sheaf of dark hair. She sat quietly with her hands in her lap.

"Just lie down. They'll be here soon to explain everything," said Mei.

Another woman arrived, then another. A fourth.

"Is all of this for me?" asked Iva Jo. "Y'all are making a fuss."

Everyone chuckled. "I'm Pam, and this is Janelle, and that's Maria. We're gonna walk you through your biopsy, Miss Iva. You ready?"

Mei would find the lump on the ultrasound.

Janelle would perform a needle biopsy on the lump.

Pam would watch over everything. The needle would hurt.

Maria would hold Iva's hand and help whoever needed assistance. A doctor would look at the ultrasound, a lab would test the biopsy sample. Iva would know soon, in a few days at most, whether it was cancer.

Hank couldn't be with her. No men. Not even the doctor. Not for this part.

The room was dim and cozy. Iva lay on a soft exam table covered in gray blankets and tried not to cry. Maria surrounded her with pillows and dimmed the lights even lower.

"When it's all over, I'll give you this," said Pam, producing a small pink disc encased in gauze. "It's a little ice pack. We'll put it on the spot where the needle goes in." Pam scrunched her nose and smiled. "I think it feels good. Nice and cool. You can keep it."

Maria put a foam block under Iva's shoulder and positioned her for the ultrasound. She untied the royal blue vest and pulled Iva's hand over her head, then stood behind her. Maria rubbed Iva's hand and forearm. Mei squirted warm goo on Iva's exposed breast and started looking for the lump.

"Will I be all right?" Iva said.

She settled her neck into her pillow. She didn't know what to do with her free hand, so she reached for her thigh, pulled at the pocket on her jeans. The ultrasound wand coasted around in the goo, beeping and looking.

Maria asked, "Are you cold? We've got extra socks."

"No thank you," said Iva. "Just don't let me get too hot. Might pass out. That's what started all this."

The wand glided to the side of Iva's breast.

"Uh-oh," said Pam. "Do you have a history of fainting?" She leaned over to look at Iva's chart. "Did we know that?"

She sighed and told the story of Margie's pottery lecture. Of the Russian girl. The tablecloth, the bowl. Meanwhile, Mei found the lump, and she and Janelle worked in tandem, cleaned her, marked a spot. As iodine sighed across her skin, Iva stared at the foam tile ceiling and felt herself sinking into the blankets, the pillows, into the goo.

"And I just . . ." said Iva. "I never understood. All that bleeding. There was so much."

Pam laughed softly. "I hate it when that happens."

Maria squeezed Iva Jo's fingers. "Yeah, I've had that, too. The Flood."

She tilted her head back to look at the women behind her. "It happened to you?"

"A couple times, right before I hit menopause," said Pam. "Nobody tells you about that part." She shrugged and smiled.

And that was all. Pam's lips were full, and her hair was coarse and unruly. From Iva's upside-down vantage point, everyone looked so plump and full in their pink and purple scrubs. They looked like berries. She thought about the Russian girl, her impossible ponytail, her impossible bright skin, her pouty lips. *So I bled*, thought Iva Jo. *It happens*.

"Pam?" she said.

"Yes, ma'am?"

"I used to work at Twitchell," said Iva. "A long time ago."

Another cold wash of iodine doused her breast. She winced.

"Oh," said Pam. She whispered to Mei, "Is that the petrochemical place over the mountain?"

Mei nodded and lowered her head.

"It was only a few years," said Iva. "I quit when I met Hank. Then I was a secretary."

"All right, honey," said Maria. "All right."

"Do you see a lot of patients who worked there?" asked Iva.

"A fair number," said Pam.

"It was good money," said Iva. "I don't tell people. Our town's pretty divided about it."

"Here comes the needle," said Janelle.

Maria squeezed Iva Jo's hand. "You might not even feel it. Some of us don't."

The pillows around Iva Jo felt thick and lush. She did not think of cancer, or of those years at Twitchell, distant years full of acrid smells and thin, clanging doors, or anything but the moment as it was.

Iva turned her head away so she wouldn't see the needle going in. A dull, distant bite pinched somewhere deep in her chest. Someone patted her shoulder, every woman hushed, and together, all together, they took a breath.

MINGO

I bought a three-dollar film camera outside Matewan the morning after Howard's daddy crashed The Box. I came out of the Rite Aid gripping it in my left hand, white plastic satchel of necessities swinging off my wrist. Howard's F-350 hulked nearby, its tires squatting wide over the line into the handicapped space. My free arm pulled the door handle above the stout red lettering: "FIELDS CONCRETE & PAVING CHARLESTON WV." I climbed in the truck and held up the throwaway.

"Clearance bin," I said, and clacked a shot of Howard holding the wheel.

"I thought you were wanting Monistat," Howard said.

He always waited in the truck when I shopped. I crinkled in the bag, past the mini-toothpaste and travel soaps, to fish out his spearmint gum. "That was last week," I said, handing him the pack. "I'm cured."

Howard stared out the windshield and opened a piece of gum without looking down. His fingers saw through packet and wrapper on their own. He laid a fine thread of cellophane in the cup holder between us and rested a powdery stick on his tongue. His gut pushed close to the steering column as he rubbed a gray patch in his goatee. Howard's face appeared meatier than usual, like he was filling out, him swelling instead of me.

"Are you old enough to remember how to use a film camera?" he said.

I balked. I'd been thirty-two since March, and Howard knew my granny never left the house without her Brownie Flash. He'd even seen some of the prints.

"You don't need to take pictures of Dad's car," he said. "Insurance'll do that."

"I just want landscapes," I said, and pointed above the strip mall to the ridge of ragged emerald behind it.

"There'll be a lot of waiting around, probably," said Howard. He popped spearmint through his front teeth. "Might as well keep yourself entertained."

We were aimed for Kentucky. No interstates bind Charleston to Harlan. Just coal country, or what used to be, and a four-lane that changes names a few times on the doglegs. In West Virginia, we had to pass through Mingo County, where I came up. The Rite Aid was a pit stop before we faced the real road. Howard pulled out of town and chewed his gum.

No surface mining wounds were visible from the highway, but I knew what was down the secondaries. Gutted mountainsides and holler fills loomed for me the whole way. Behind every ridge lay some smothered or poisoned creek, some thick scar of geological mastectomy. My chest slumped; the loss laid into me like it does everyone who knew the place before.

I didn't speak to my husband. Some gaggle of carpetbaggers was plotting an airport at a reclaim site here. Howard was going to pour their columns, pave two lots. When he got the airport contract back in April, I gave him a lecture against mountaintop removal mining. "Overburden," I had reminded him. That's what they called what they stole. I told him he'd be taking money from rapers of the land. It was stone-cold collusion, I said.

"Well, they're gonna pay somebody, why not us? Why not the people who've lost out?" he'd said.

"You didn't lose anything," I said over and over. The baby was still in me then, and I was dreaming of curved earth every night. "I grew up there, not you."

I was appeased by the idea of coming down from Charleston with him. Usually I just stayed in our garage office and filed payroll. But when he took the airport contract, Howard said I could ride with him into Mingo County every now and then. I made plans. I'd walk in the weeds near my grandmother's house, breathe homey air while he signed invoices and flagged mixer trucks. Mingo didn't need an airport, just like it hadn't needed a golf course, but they'd plow one out anyhow for the few suits who still came through. Nobody had a plane, so this enterprise would surely fail and suck a little life out of the killers and capitalists. That I would watch.

Only once, in early May, did I visit the airport site. High up, on a dusty, counterfeit expanse where hundreds of acres of lush mountain used to be, Howard flagged trucks and negotiated. The missing forest tingled in me like phantom limbs. Being there brought on my morning sickness. I knelt deep into the quease. My fingers touched chalky gravel instead of loam, and I shut my eyes to what they'd gouged out.

Soon after, I had reason to stay home for Howard's trips into Mingo. I didn't even make it past my first trimester this time; I stayed in the city and bled through the spring. The second one was easier. It was simpler to fail early, to empty out without having yet felt a sense of fullness. Howard said again, we'll try again. I pretended that was true and shut my mouth.

***

Over the Kentucky border, the view was less painful. Summer had come in thick this year. Howard eased us over the state line, and both of us sighed a full breath. Kentucky had cleaner money—at least by my standards. Years back some scrappy plutocrat, somebody Howard's daddy hadn't voted for, pulled strings in the capital and laced a web of bone-colored state highways through all the snaking hollers. On this half of our drive, there was more freshness in the hills.

Kentucky hadn't let their mountains alone. Mining companies blasted off just as many ridgetops here as in West Virginia, but here they kept the cuts hidden deeper, gashed hills farther from public view. With the preserved elevations and pale roads, any trip through Pike and Harlan Counties dizzies the rider. Highways in eastern Kentucky run low between mountains like half-buried bones. White gullies through the green. On 119, Howard marveled at all the concrete, the square bridges, the engineering. I looked up past numbered signs, up to kudzu on high, and imagined myself inside a hedge maze in some far-off, castle-rich country.

Howard wasn't going to talk about this accident, his daddy's fourth in a year. Not to me. I'd already screamed my piece about Hassel still driving. Hassel had no business. Ever since he'd been widowed, his menace had amplified. The old man had torn up three sedans in the last half decade, dinging fenders, tumbling over berms, and once almost driving straight through the sliding doors of the Dollar Pik. Each time, Howard found a way to make excuses for not taking his father's keys. With each crash, my knees locked tighter, and my voice got flatter when I fumed.

Howard's daddy was a Harlan man. Hassel Fields came from about the same conditions I had. He raised his children off the profits from his corner IGA back when coal money still streamed through town. By the time Hassel closed his store and retired, Harlan County was in decline, and his children had packed off to big-town college and condo. Hassel timed everything just right, and Howard couldn't face him winding down. If his daddy lost his power, then Howard would have to reconcile with that, and with me. So he either tuned me out or told me some way we were alike, my father-in-law and I. And so the man kept driving.

I kicked off so much about Hassel being a public threat that Howard's sister wouldn't talk to me anymore, either. Not after she told me she wouldn't let her youngest ride in the car with her own father anymore. I'd already had enough of Violet, with her organic garden and her high shoulders, always acting like I was a superstition she no longer believed. My sister-in-law taught macroeconomics at some hippie school outside Lexington. I didn't give a shit.

"You won't let Samuel ride with his granddaddy?" I said to her.

The boy was in her lap chasing birds on her phone. He was three, all soft down, with little pudgy arms like stacks of fresh marshmallows.

"No," she said. "It is a worry."

We were in her kitchen, visiting on a Saturday. There's a big interstate between Charleston and Lexington, so the trip takes half as long as it does to Harlan. Howard loves kids; he was always missing his niece and nephews. We visited my sister-in-law more than Hassel, more than my people in Mingo. He hadn't wanted to move to West Virginia, but work was work.

"I'll find a way to talk around it so Dad doesn't realize." She smoothed her boy's downy hair, looked back at me. "We have to love him through this, you know? It's so difficult, I think, to lose one's autonomy. Driving is all he's got left."

Violet went on, but I quit listening halfway through that mess.

"So it's fine if old Hassel flies around town in his little boxy car and kills somebody's baby," I said, "just as long as it's not *your* baby."

And then I crinkled my nose and nodded how the pretty girls in middle school used to when they picked on the kids from over my way. I learned her kind's code a long time ago, and I used it on her now. She knew why.

My sister-in-law's eyes got big, and behind me Howard said, "Tina."

I held off saying more. Violet knew what it meant to hold tight to her own child right in front of me. She went quiet. Now she doesn't talk to me, and Howard shuts down when I try to say Hassel Fields is a danger. No matter; I hadn't gone on the last few weekend visits to Lexington anyhow. I'd been busy lately hollowing out.

***

We crossed into Harlan County after an hour of listening to the A/C exhale between us. I'd only made Howard stop once, somewhere near Pikeville, so I could snap a shot with my little camera. I spied some kudzu choking a church sign that read "You Shall Know Them By Their Fruit—Hardburly First Baptist." It spoke to me, that verse amongst the coiling leaves, so I told him to pull over. I couldn't explain my fascination with the sign, so I said I was taking pictures of roadkill. Nearby, a squished whistlepig splayed in the sun, teats up, fur glued to blacktop. She reeked of heat and rotted earth. I aimed and clicked at her, and at the kudzu, back and forth, while Howard waited in the pickup's cooled cabin.

As we closed the distance to the low-slung hospital where his daddy was sleeping off the morphine, Howard asked me about yeast infections.

"How often do you get them?"

"I mean, maybe once a year? Not as much as some."

"Is it a chemistry thing?" he said. He crunched his temples into crow's feet. "Like a—like I don't know, a sign of something not being balanced in there?" He nodded at my crotch.

I tightened my lips to a white line. "That is not the reason it happened," I said.

"I didn't say it was," said Howard. "I'm saying, is it the other way around?"

He took his gum out at the traffic light, folded it neatly into its old wrapper, and tucked the wad in the cupholder. "The stress, those antidepressants you take. Maybe all this effort to get pregnant is—I don't know. Upsetting the balance. Maybe you need to let go of things a little."

"Howard," I said. "It was just an itchy cooch. It's July. It's hot."

He pulled into the hospital lot and sighed, patted his open palms against the wheel three times. "Well, let's get on in there. Find out what the old man's done to himself."

Harlan Hospital was modern and beige, with plain angles and no design. Duke Power or US Steel probably built it out of guilt, with a sack of cash thrown over the company's shoulder on their way out of town. I marked the Methodist church across the street, brick and proud. It had the confident architectural details of the WPA days. The two buildings stared at each other.

Harlan was sturdy. I thought so on every visit. Harlan County had rock under it my Mingo towns couldn't muster. And dovetail corners and craftsman bungalows Lexington and Charleston had forgotten or remodeled.

I hated Harlan. Every time we came here, I wanted to stay. The land felt impenetrable and pristine. I wanted to swim in the black Kentucky dirt to prove it wrong, take my revenge on it. Mingo was barren, and Charleston was strange. Somehow I decided the blame lay here.

I flopped out of the cab and swung my canvas purse strap crossways over my chest, then fished the tossaway camera out of the satchel. I snapped a picture of a rank of ambulances parked in a line in the distance, then snapped a shot of the WPA church, then the dull, square mouth of glass at the hospital's entrance. I wound the nubbly black wheel and pulled the film forward with my thumb. It was a familiar motion, and my tendon tightened like a child's.

I held the camera as we entered the gray glass doors. My sister-in-law was waiting for us. She grabbed her brother's bicep and leaned into him, spoke my name. Howard said, "All right now, Violet," and stroked her back in a circle. She turned to lead us to their father.

The hallways were cool and bland, a maze of sameness. The medicinal hush deepened as we neared Hassel's room. Even wounded, the old man still had the whole ward spooked. My sister-in-law eased up to his door and called softly. I kept back, third in line. Howard and his sister wavered, stepped in slow. I peeked in just once, around Howard's left side, to take in the damage.

Hassel was a heap, and weak. I caught sight of him as a thick-armed mound of fabric and tubes at the center of the room, his face the only stark notion in the sterile tableau. At least two white sheets were tossed over his brawn. He was propped up, glaring. A crimson welt from the airbag's punch bloomed across his left jowl. He nodded at me.

"Tina," he said.

He put weight into my name. I tilted up the tossaway in my slack hand and shot a surreptitious portrait of Hassel. I used my thigh to muffle the click.

I receded to the waiting area while Howard and his sister sank further in. Outside Hassel's room, four seats faced each other on a neat trapezoid of dark-blue carpet. Their cushions smelled like bleach and cheap shoes, and a scatter of magazines littered the table between them. My sister-in-law had only brought her two eldest: her girl Mabel, who was all wiry limbs and a nest of hair, and teenaged Eric, who kept silent. He slouched sideways, back to his grandfather's door, moonfaced and pubescent above a lighted screen. No sign of little Samuel with those marshmallow arms.

I sat across from Eric, facing Hassel's room, and felt glad I wouldn't have to babysit these two much. Their mother bustled in and out across the narrow hall while Howard lingered inside the room. His voice and his father's mingled into a drone. Little Mabel sat beside me reading a puzzle book. She giggled now and then about The Box while I flipped through last year's tabloids and tried to keep the resinous chair arms from pinching my skin.

We called Hassel's car The Box because it was a cheap white cube of a thing, mostly plastic. He had once captained only stalwart chassis with steel dashboards. The Box was all he could afford after so many crashes, all the State Farm agent would insure. The Box had been Hassel's last shot. Now it was crumpled up, totaled, impounded at a junk lot out near the county line. Looked like Howard's daddy wasn't a driving man anymore; I'd been corroborated.

Howard emerged from his conversation with Hassel with a glower. My sister-in-law stood in the corridor and debriefed him in a low, even whisper while I sat with her kids. The cops had taken Hassel's license at the scene; he had a court date, misdemeanors to contend. He'd jacked into some attorney's spendy coupe, so that was that.

Mabel plopped off her chair and skipped up to me. She turned over the tossaway camera in my lap, ran her finger across its edge, and put a hand on my knee. "Aunt Tina?"

I was wearing thick jeans, and I felt the warmth of her palm through the dark cloth. She tucked her little elbow into her side and swayed, head cocked. She was going on six.

"Are you and Uncle Howard still having a baby?"

I told the child no and ruffled my magazine. I pulled the pages to my chest in a wad and dropped my gaze. My sister-in-law flitted up while I stared at the linoleum. A vague, wax-buffed reflection of Howard swung toward Hassel's door, then back toward me.

"Mabel, honey," she said. She knelt down to her girl and reached out to pat the older boy's sneaker. "Why don't we let Auntie have some time with Papaw?" Then she shooed both kids off to the Arby's for lunch.

Howard cleared his throat twice. I looked up after the children were gone, just as he lowered his head and said, "Well, I'm going to the junkyard to have a gander at that Box."

I sat still, observing, as a scene change played out for me with theatrical rhythm. As soon as everyone had limped down the hall stage left, the PT rounded the corner opposite and glided up to Hassel's open door like some kind of dancer.

"Mr. Fields?" The PT tapped on the door and nudged it open. "I'm Walter. Your physical therapist."

Walter looked like he belonged on a bottle of bathroom cleaner. He was shaved bald, green eyed, and his scrubs hung sharp over the tightest set of muscles I'd ever seen. He slipped into Hassel's room, and I straightened my back, leaned forward to hear.

The PT went through a litany of questions and coaxed my father-in-law out into the hallway. Hassel emerged, rumpled and pained, gripping an aluminum walker. I stood as they came out and made to join them.

"Hassel, you all right?" I said, and eased up alongside.

The old man huffed, and gripped the walker's side handles tighter.

"Tolerable," he said. He tilted his head at me and said to Walter, "My daughter-in-law. Come down from Mingo."

He didn't look at either of us; he just started shuffling off like he had errands. I wondered whether he knew I missed Mingo County or had just forgotten where his son and I lived now.

Walter nodded brightly and said, "I want to watch him walk? Check his range of motion, study his gait. You can tag along; tell me if you notice anything unusual. You know his movements better than I do."

I walked the hallway with them. Walter asked Hassel questions. He kept his hands close, arced and tense, waiting to catch the old man if he buckled. Hassel would have none of it. He behaved as if the PT wasn't there and willed himself forward, refusing Walter's touch. Somewhere in the slow route they took together, Walter decided I was Hassel's best chance at recovery. Whenever the old man blamed his hearing and wouldn't heed, Walter spoke to me.

"He's got to practice using a walker," he said. "See how he's putting weight on his elbows?"

Just then Hassel stopped short and began to wobble. Walter's biceps flexed as he turned from me and swooped in to steady his patient. Hassel's body righted under Walter's power, and he pressed on. The old man didn't know it wasn't his own strength; that's how easy Walter held him as they inched down the hall's perimeter. Hassel's left arm brushed the pale pink walls, and the walker's rubber feet squeaked and scuffed the tile. The old man kept flapping his hand to be released, smacking the walker forward while his flanks rattled under his gown. Eventually Walter relented, left the old man to his sloppy progress, and chatted to me.

"So you're from Mingo County?" he said.

"Yeah, but we live in Charleston now. My husband's from here."

"Well, tell me about it," he said. "I got a cousin who used to work up there a long time ago."

Hassel continued on his path away from us.

"There's nothing there," I said. "Used to be, though."

"Were your people miners?"

I shook my head. "My daddy was a preacher. He died when I was young."

"Amen," said Walter.

"Hardly," I replied, and Walter smirked.

We both crossed our arms and watched Hassel puff and hobble.

"I like coming through Kentucky," I said. "Harlan's nice, don't you think?"

Walter chuffed. "Boy, you must really come from the back of nothing if you think Harlan's worth a compliment."

My forehead went hot, and Walter put out a soft hand. "I didn't mean—" he said.

I shrugged. Walter was probably right. Most likely I had east Kentucky figured wrong. Things were probably just as bad here as they were in Mingo, as bad as they were all over.

"We've got a house in Charleston," I said. "It's big, four bedrooms. We make out all right." I looked up at the foam tile ceiling, pictured downtown Harlan. "Guess I just see this place as having character."

Hassel grunted his way past a janitorial cart and cursed.

"In-laws notwithstanding," I added.

"Naturally," Walter said with a bow, and moved back across the hall to resume his duties.

Walter kept his hands out, gently poised, as he counted out a rhythm for the old man to walk to. Left, right, good, good. He had one tattoo on the inside of his left wrist—a plain circle around a feather. I remembered the tossaway in my back pocket and wished I could fill up the roll with stolen pictures of Walter's toned arms, but he'd surely catch the aperture's click and think me even weirder. I committed that tattoo to memory while Hassel lied to Walter and said he was fine, fine to drive, fine to get himself back to bed, fine to set his own pace.

Walter finally deferred, cast his inked arm out with a theatrical flourish, and left Hassel in the hallway. On his way out, I told him I'd make sure Hassel got back to bed. I thanked those muscles as they passed. He smiled and said, "All in a day's work, Mountaineer."

The old man hauled himself back to his room in record time; agitation charged his batteries.

After I saw Hassel back to bed, I fidgeted for twenty minutes alone, then roamed down to the snack machines beyond the nurse's station. I was fishing in my pocket for a dollar when Walter reappeared alongside me with a clipboard and a puffy blue lunch sack.

"On my break," he said.

He pulled in close and let his arm brush my waist while he bought us each a lemon-lime soda. The hallway stood empty and bright around us, and I saw myself reflected in the candy-vending glass—pixie cut, T-shirt and jeans, jagged at the joints. At a squint, you'd have thought I was a boy. Howard was taking a while at the

junk lot, reviewing the wreckage of The Box. Hassel was in bed
trying not to look winded. And my sister-in-law was still at Arby's
smugging over her brood.

"Your father-in-law is—" He reached for his change out of the
machine, shook his head. "He's a tough case."

Walter confided in me. I was kin to the patient, after all, and he
seemed worn down by his shift. Hassel has that effect. His face was
still, but a cord in his neck popped as he spoke. Hassel, Walter said,
must not drive. They would let him go home today, but he needed
watching and shouldn't live alone. Somebody was going to have
to dress him. Catastrophe was imminent. At his age, the strengths
he'd long trusted having failed him, Hassel would fall badly, break
bones. Hassel could barely manage a flat hallway, wouldn't listen to
instructions. He thought feebleness was a state of mind. Walter had
seen this brand of defiance before, never with a good end.

I agreed. Yes. To everything. To everything Walter said about
Hassel being disabled. Somebody finally saw it. This PT was giving
me ammo, a line of proof that Hassel was unfit, spent. Each word
swelled me up with righteous certainty that my sister-in-law was a
pushover, Hassel needed taming and brute care, and Howard wasn't
paying attention to any of it. Not one important thing around him
was my husband looking in the eye.

"The family," I said to Walter's arms, to the fine motor skills of
his person, "doesn't want to admit it. But I know." I chucked my
head in the general direction of the Arby's. "They keep drawing
the curtain."

"I see that a lot," said Walter.

"I went through it with my granny. We held firm until she quit
bucking. She passed easier for it," I said. "The Fields don't know
how to do that. They can't face facts."

He nodded, frowned, and pushed out his clipboard to show me
a form he'd been filling out—a medical assessment with a copy of
the police accident report attached.

"This'll make its way to the DMV. I promise you." Walter was reporting Hassel to the state.

"The DMV? Will he lose his license? Permanently?"

Walter nodded. The soda machine's fridge motor clicked on, and the hallway rumbled for a moment. My fingers moved to find his inky feather. I clutched his arm and nodded, kept nodding until my head collided into his shoulder. Walter stood firm.

I gripped my cola bottle against my chest. "Hassel could kill someone if he drives again."

Walter grunted a yes and touched his hand to the small of my back. I flinched at first; then some brittle wire inside me snapped.

"We've been trying to have a baby," I said. "I've lost two."

Walter's arm circled in tighter. He grimaced at the floor, and his free hand gripped his clipboard. I tried to laugh, but instead I began to shake and blubber. I leaned into him.

"Howard's sperm swim just fine, but I can't seem to catch them right." I sniffed in snot and grinned, then lost my nerve again and whimpered into Walter's bicep. "We don't talk about it."

Walter stroked his hand up and placed it onto my shoulder. His hand weighed as much as my marriage, just that small piece of him.

"It's hard," he said. "Of course."

"What if Hassel was to kill somebody, driving like he does? They won't hear. They don't listen." I closed my eyes, gripped the thin plastic bottle until it crackled and caved in my hand.

Walter passed his hand down my arm. My skin had been clay all morning, all year, but now it tingled. My vision blurred as I welled up a second time and leaned harder against him.

Right then Violet swanned in, backlit, at the end of the hall. Her children skittered past us. As she took in the sight of me curled and weepy under Walter's care, her shoulders slumped. She blinked and shifted her focus as if she'd seen me unclothed. I recoiled from Walter and walked dutifully toward her. My skin went clay and cold again. I dried my face, stuffed the soda bottle in my purse, and ducked Walter's gaze.

Violet's voice was tight. "We've got to get Dad ready. He's been discharged." She handed me a white paper bag. "We got you a roast beef. Mabel thought you'd be hungry."

She put a hand under my elbow, guiding me as if I were blind, and together we went back to Hassel.

***

The ward nurse had told us Hassel couldn't dress himself, so I had good reason when I refused to give him his clothes. Violet was at the nurse's station asking about pills and doses. She asked me to check on the old man. I reeled through his door still in a dazzle of emotion. The room's medicinal reek revived me like a smelling salt, and my breath came in gulps.

Hassel filled up his bed like a hickory stump. I put a hand on my chest and tilted one hip, trying not to face him down too hard.

"Well, Dad," I said, casual like. "You gonna make it?"

Hassel nodded, then flung his torso forward. "I'm ready to go," he said.

"They'll send somebody to help you," I said. I was still snotty and worn through from weeping into Walter's muscles. "Just hold on now, and let them get you dressed."

Hassel grunted. He rocked his bottom back and forth, inching his feet off the bed onto the cold floor. Sheets and gown swirled around him.

"I'm not waiting, Tina," he said through rocks in his throat. "I want to get on home." He pointed behind me. "Reach me my shirt and pants out of that cabinet and bring them here."

"Hassel, you've got to have help," I said. "You heard the PT say you don't have any balance. You'll fall over pulling on your underwear."

Hassel seared his rheumy pupils at me and pointed again, fist quaking.

"Pants," he said.

I breathed. My arms felt sore and soft, like they feel after chopping wood in the cold.

"No, sir," I said.

My fight hadn't left me, and Hassel knew it. We stared each other down like frontier outlaws. The room swelled with his ire.

Hassel didn't test me further. He would have if I'd been one of his own. Instead, after three tries, he spluttered up off the bed. Once standing, he lowered his chin and glared at me through spidery eyebrows. Fluorescent light pooled around a clutter of charts and bedpans beside him.

"Fine, then, young lady," he said.

Then Hassel Fields, all eighty-three shaky years of him, pulled off his hospital gown with an operatic reveal. His flabby arms swooped up, and after a defiant fumble, he stood before me buck naked, daring me to stop him from seizing his khakis.

My breath fell out of me in a whoosh, and my hands dropped to my sides. I loosed the Arby's bag, which flopped to the floor and landed on my foot. I gawked.

Hassel's splotched, veiny body was a fearsome map. He had two long, black bruises where The Box's seatbelt had spared his life— one near his heart, the other across his belly. His ball sack hung low and full like a finch sock. His legs looked scrawny and pale under the bulk of his battered torso.

Every muscle in me stilled. I couldn't move. Here was Howard's source, and here was I refusing it. My secondary brain, a layer of sentience underneath the immediate, compared his body to my husband's and cast me into the future. *If I stay with Howard*, I thought, *this is what I'll be contending with in thirty years.*

Hassel advanced toward me, dick wobbling, mumbling in want of a shirt. His breath was even now, like a steam train. I fumble-grabbed a dirty blanket hanging off the chair to my right, but I couldn't think how to stop his advance. I held the blanket wide and moved weakly to trap him in it, as if he were a beast I had to net. Then his gait hitched. His gnarled toes splayed, and his eyes reeled. He put a hand out into thin air and hunkered weight into his heels to balance himself. I watched his naked body veer toward toppling, then just barely right itself. Hassel gave a little bounce in his knees and lowered his shoulders like a scolded child.

The tension dropped out of my muscles, and my shock evaporated. I thought about my recent stints in similar sanitized rooms, how nurses force vulnerability upon a woman with their needle drips and saccharine coos, and I felt doused with pity. Hassel was helpless.

I planted my feet, tightened my glutes, and bent in to swaddle him. I held the blanket aloft, baby blue. I arced my hands and swooped the blanket around him like I was making to waltz. His shoulders were granite, and he still glared, so I tried to chortle and soothe.

"Hassel," I said, soft as I could.

My hands sunk into him. I eased forward. The old man smelled like iodine and mildew. I said his name again and gripped my hands tighter, feeling for his cool flesh through the blanket.

"Come on now, honey," I said. "You can show off all you want, but I'm still going to—"

"Dad!" my sister-in-law gasped.

She'd come in with the children just in time to see us in our freakish pose, me embracing her father's front half in a rumpled blanket, his whole back side exposed, both of us a wall facing the other. Little Mabel squealed, and Eric muttered "Dude" and turned his face away.

Violet flitted up and pushed me aside, livid with modesty. Hassel pointed to his clothes, instructed. I stepped back, suddenly hungry for the sandwich I'd dropped. She did his bidding in a quiet state of terror that made me feel briefly sorry for her. In return, Hassel allowed his daughter to cover him. I gathered up my Arby's bag, flopped in the Naugahyde chair by the window, and watched them all fuss around while I nibbled on my roast beef.

While his shirt was being buttoned, Hassel turned toward me. His cheeks softened, and he gave me a slow wink. I stopped mid-chew and raised my eyebrows at him.

Howard walked in a few seconds later clutching a stack of insurance forms. He stopped sharp, sensing the tension in the room.

"What happened?" he said to Violet.

Hassel fanned away his son's offered hand and eased himself onto his mechanized mattress. His shirt skewed over his top half like a messy kerchief. Unzipped trousers hitched and splayed their pockets over his bottom. His daughter knelt before him, holding a beige sock in each hand. They looked to me like unlubed rubbers.

"Your wife wouldn't give me my clothes," he said to Howard. His nostrils whistled as his left sock went on, and fluorescent light sparkled off a sliver of hazel in his eye. "So I gave her a memory."

He stared into Howard's drooped mouth and told his daughter not to tie his shoes too tight. The air felt dense, and I heard someone retch out in the hallway.

Hassel's face blossomed into a grin, and he cut the silence with a massive wheeze. Then another. His shoulders clenched and loosened with each rasp. His bruised, tender belly pulled in, then shoved out in quickening contractions. His lips and eyes widened with bitter delight. From my corner, I began to quake in my seat. I threw my head back and inhaled, felt my guts burble, and soon the pair of us synchronized into guffaws.

We were merciless. We went slack and leaned over howling. We cackled for a solid minute. I wailed, and Hassel let out exhausted whoops and kept wiping his eyes. Violet stood up, pulled her children to her, and filed up next to Howard. The four of them formed a line opposite us, blocking the door. They watched our hysterics with horrified stares. After their silence pushed us back hard enough, Hassel and I settled into hitched giggles, and the Fields gang slowly unclenched. The children were hushed. Howard chopped off the last of our glee.

"Tina," he said. His arms were crossed, and his mirror sunglasses glowed atop his spiky, gelled hair. "Why don't you go wait in the truck."

I rose, slung my purse over my shoulder, and quit the room. In the doorway I looked back at Hassel and pistoled my thumb and forefinger at his chest. The old man closed his eyes. I walked out, tossed the Arby's bag in a hazardous waste bin, and left the Fields family to bustle like drones over their queen. The tossaway rattled against my ass in my back pocket, and I wished I'd thought to take a snapshot of Howard's and Violet's faces.

The sun smacked into me as I left the building. Our F-350 was parked beside a median of dark Kentucky grass. I walked past the truck, put my back to it, and stopped on the median. I squatted in the hot grass and let it itch my ankles under the cuffs of my jeans. I pulled the camera out of my back pocket and tossed it into my bag. The WPA church across the way faced me. I nodded to it, and the red bricks asked me point-blank whether I wanted a divorce. I shrugged.

Howard had brought me out of Mingo, saved me when I was just rounding twenty, so I couldn't fault him. For all that I pined about it, my home county didn't have anything to stay for or go back to. The mining reclaim sites, scarred like they were, couldn't imitate old ground. Suits and invaders had dumped toxic dirt onto what they blasted out, leaving the hillsides false, silent slumps. The curving bulge and teem, the mountains we used to stare off to as kids, were now corpses stuffed with dirty packing foam. A new airport. Who needed a plane to nowhere? Mingo was lost, laid bare. Marrying Howard meant I escaped the worst.

If it came down to it, I saw I'd be the one who moved in with

Hassel and kept care of him. Violet was busy with her children and all of Lexington, and my husband was no nursemaid. Hassel and me had the same destiny, and I would wipe his ass and drive us both on reckless errands over white Kentucky roads. There was no other task for me to take on. I had submitted to the same indignities he had, knew the same country. Howard was right; there were similarities.

We would most likely bed down at the Super 8, then head back to Charleston the next day to regroup. We'd decide there, while his father's pain settled, whether either of us would say any of what was on my mind.

I had begun to sweat when Walter the PT swaggered out a side door by the ambulance rank. He stopped some distance away on another grassy median. He turned eastward, away from me and the WPA church, and lit a cigarette under the shade of a small maple. I stood up and slunk against the truck's bumper. Then I fished my keys out, climbed in the cab on the passenger side, and cranked the engine and A/C.

A wall of cool pushed me back in my seat. Walter smoked on, and with each puff, his back flexed. My hands found the tossaway in my purse. I pulled it out and set it on the dash. I held back from the viewfinder a whole arm's stretch, afraid to put eye to lens. I aimed the camera at Walter. I wanted a shot of his arms, his fine feather, his circle of ink.

I clicked away at him. Between snaps, I could swear I felt an egg slip from me and glide down to the gusset of my lace briefs. I thumbed the nubbly black wheel until I remembered I didn't know of a Rite Aid back home in Charleston, or in Mingo, or anywhere else, that still developed real film. I'd have to hunt to find somebody who could process the negatives.

I pulled the camera down off the dash and held it in my lap. The F-350 rumbled and yawned, and I began clicking off shots, photos of nothing. Dashboard, lap, wind, click, to the end of the reel. I'd most likely lay the camera to rest in the nightstand, undeveloped. The truck's windshield was bug spattered and tinted, so likely my pictures would never come out anyway.

Walter flicked his butt into a hedge and went inside through the glass doors. His shoulders looked narrower from a distance. Maybe Hassel was tougher than him after all. Kentucky sure was.

I cracked my window and squeezed the tossaway tight in my right hand for a long moment. Then I flung it out of the cab. The camera twirled in a long arc across the median and landed in a patch of soil under a laurel. The truck idled. I pulled my knees to my chest, balled my body tight, and leaned against the door. I waited for Howard, but I didn't look for him. I clenched my hands under my chin, and I wished for Mingo to be put back the way it had been, wished Hassel could drive himself home in a grand, fine wagon. Hot summer air seeped into the truck. I curled myself deeper, gripped my shins, and stared hard out my window, waiting to see.

FROGS

$\mathcal{A}$ decade ago, summer was full of their mating calls. But now—"
The naturalist tilted his head. His long neck sprouted wiry cords of muscle, and his voice sank into the soft dark.

"He's really feeling it," Frank whispered in his sister's ear.

"Hush," said Carolyn. "I can't hear."

The naturalist's hands were long-fingered and delicate. He swooped up with his right one to make a grand gesture at the clear twilight sky lowering like a blanket over the forest, while his left hand kept his flashlight pointing downward. Under the milky strands of emerging starlight, his hands looked like bat's wings— fine boned, claw-like. His whole body was thin, his eyes large and dark. The naturalist was altogether like a bat.

"But as we have discussed in our previous lectures, for those of you who attended . . ." Here the naturalist paused for effect.

Frank and Carolyn looked at the ground. They had not attended any of the previous lectures at the biological station, and everyone seemed to know it. An earnest-looking nine-year-old girl with two crooked braids twisted up her mouth and gave them both a long, disapproving up-and-down. Frank and Carolyn did not have the proper clothing or tools; they did not know where to stand. They did not smell of the organic ginger bug repellant all the other attendees used.

"... if you recall from those previous discussions, the ongoing calamities visited upon the biodiversity in our region have hit the families Hylidae and Ranidae hardest. We hear far fewer frogs than we used to. Our nights are quieter than they should be."

The naturalist paused again. Something rustled in the bush behind him and let out a small, doleful peep.

He pointed a solitary finger in the air to acknowledge the peep, which had the effect of holding everyone in silence for some moments. The trees at the edge of the clearing held still and thick for him, too. For no discernible reason, except that in groups of people, random subgroups often form and move together, five or six of the twenty souls present looked upwards and pondered their altitude. Carolyn was among them. She clutched her brochure to her chest and traced her eyes along the inky border between the tops of trees and the night sky. She listened for frogs while Frank shifted and yawned behind her.

The biological station sat at five thousand feet, secluded at the top of a mountain ridge far above the small university that operated it. The school purchased the hundred acres of high-country forest land in the 1950s, and it had been used as a research site ever since. According to the program brochure and the assorted gossip of regular visitors to the station, the naturalist was an adjunct botany instructor at the university, but he spent most of his time waiting for the school year to end. He would then abandon the valley of tenured outsiders and frat houses to return to the mossy, misty solitude of the station. He was its longest-running resident; no one could remember him not being here.

Twice a week, from late April to mid-August, there were lectures on various topics. Members of the public were invited if they registered in advance and made a donation. Students and university faculty got in free. The naturalist would, during these visiting hours, summon the energy to be barely sociable. Otherwise, for the rest of the summer, it was him, a few graduate assistants, and the amphibians, mammals, birds, trees, and plants of the Southern Highlands. His longevity at the biological station and lack of outside commitments resulted in a general consensus that the naturalist was a genius, and that he had earned the right to hold forth on matters even outside his area of academic expertise.

Those who attended lectures were respectful of the station's wild inhabitants, and of the naturalist. Few spoke. The children who came here were often escorted by stolid grandparents who suppressed the children's giddy wiggling. Sometimes the children themselves dragged their parents in a fit of juvenile scientific curiosity, and so were better behaved than their elders. Hardly anyone poked the turtles or picked the flowers. The naturalist often remarked that he believed the effort it took to get here weeded out the people who would do such things. The station and the narrow road that ended at its gravel parking lot were rugged, only partially plotted in GPS devices and online maps. The signposts were small, minimally informative. Nature thinned the herd. Only those who had the persistence to find the station, and the quiet certainty to hike the steep, dark trail up from where they'd parked, ever made it here.

Frank slapped his arm and cursed. In the broken silence, someone handed him a bottle of organic bug repellant. He squirted himself and stuck his now ginger-scented hand back out into the darkness for someone to reclaim their bottle. It disappeared mysteriously, in such a gentle way that Frank did not speak his thanks.

"If no one has questions, we'll move on to the nature walk."

No one had questions. The naturalist seemed pleased. He pointed his flashlight upwards and began to stroll out of the clearing toward a heavily canopied path at the far end of the bio station's courtyard. A few flashlights bounced off the small collection of buildings to their right—two labs, a rustic staff dormitory, and a small museum, all closed now. It was nearly nine; full dark loomed.

The naturalist turned at the last moment, just before entering the woods, and announced to his followers, "We may lose each other."

The crowd paused for his next instruction.

"If that happens," he continued, "all the research trails eventually end here"—he staked his beam at a patch of courtyard grass—"or at the parking area. Just make your way back to your vehicle. You all have your flashlights and your pictorial brochures, so please proceed quietly. Listen and watch to identify tonight's featured species, and stay on the trail at all times."

Carolyn and Frank found each other's hands as they proceeded with the group into the woods. They each noted the coolness of the other's skin, a surprise in the May darkness.

"Don't lose me," Carolyn squeaked.

Frank squeezed his sister's fingers.

Twins. They were thirty-seven. Carolyn had gained weight since her divorce, and so had recently taken up hiking. Frank worked at the paper mill in town, the one the university activists called a scourge and kept trying to close. The one tourists complained about because of its industrial smells, its unsightly smokestack interrupting their mountain views.

Carolyn and Frank had lived in the mountains all their lives. They had moved in together after Carolyn's divorce. Both were childless. Neither knew anything about local ecology.

The only time Frank went hiking was in the summer when Carolyn made him do it instead of tubing at Deep Creek, or when his ex-brother-in-law felt like hunting deer. Frank did not own a gun, but he thought his ex-brother-in-law was a better man than him, so he always tagged along when invited. He would borrow a rifle, chat to loud local boys about weather and ammunition. He never killed anything. Frank liked venison, but Carolyn wouldn't cook it. "Because of Bambi," she would say, pouting. Carolyn did not like Frank hanging out with her ex-husband.

Other than that, their relationship, their twinship, worked fine. It worked just fine.

Ahead of them, a family of four were whispering earnestly into a stack of wet rocks. Their youngest child had found a salamander.

The girl with the crooked braids breezed past and said, "Salamanders were last week. We're not even in the *real* woods yet."

Chastened, the family straightened themselves and continued walking.

The path soon enfolded itself into dense forest and carried Frank and Carolyn slowly higher. Trees and brush pulled closer into one another, as if the vegetation regarded the path as an inconvenient interruption in the mingled conversation of their leaves. Calls of animals awakening for nocturnal hunts buzzed in the distance, a distance that seemed nearer occasionally, when a lone squawk or rustle burst just out of flashlight range. In the purpling gloom, Carolyn paused and breathed.

"Earth," said Carolyn with reverence. "It smells so earthy. Don't you just love dirt?"

They carried on for a little while. The group's flashlights made eerie pools of light around them—a man's leg, glowing and pink, the chop of a harsh beam across black stone—but their lights could not reach far. Cool dark embraced each follower like a caul.

No one had any sense of time except for the passage of heavy purple into true blackness as they deepened into woods, evening, night. The naturalist led them along, far ahead, making no noise as he walked. He made no effort to interact with the group.

Occasionally someone asked a hushed question, but the naturalist did not always answer. Only if he approved of the question, only when the naturalist had something specific to explain, would he speak. He signaled the group that he was about to hold forth by pausing his loping gait and moving his head in a slow, graceful

S pattern. This gesture held a certain portent that always silenced the group, even if they could not see him from where they stood.

Frank's hands were fidgety tonight, and he reached for the brochure in his pocket. He curled the paper, turning it over and over until he had made a tight tube with the paper. He batted the tube against his fingers, making sharp, rapid thuds. The noise made him feel better somehow, less lost in the dark. Ahead, the naturalist stopped short, half turned, then quickly walked on, clearly perturbed at this unnatural sound. Someone shushed Frank, and the group continued following their leader. Frank stuffed the brochure tube back into his pocket and paused to let his unseen shusher pass by.

Frank stood perpendicular to the trail, his size thirteen feet spread wide, staring into the middle distance, shoulders slightly forward, mouth open. Carolyn approached him and peered closely at his posture in the darkness. He was a stocky man, and he wore an orange University of Tennessee T-shirt that did his round belly no favors. Frank rarely left the house without a baseball cap clamped onto his skull, and tonight he had selected one that advertised his favorite beer. The sporty, reflective polygons of his sunglasses rested on the brim. Carolyn watched him, watched him breathing in the dark, his goatee framing his round, open mouth.

"Are we rednecks?" she asked.

"What?" Frank turned his head. "No. We're not hippies like these people"—Frank nodded to the group ahead of them on the trail—"but I'm no hick. Go on ahead now."

Carolyn moved on while Frank took a moment to himself. Eventually he sucked in his gut and trudged to catch up with the group. The naturalist had paused to admonish everyone about shining their flashlights into the trees.

"Be selective. Discriminating," he entreated them. "Our beams may frighten the frogs and make them go quiet. Madame, please extinguish your headlamp."

Almost everyone switched off their lights, choosing to proceed blindly from then on. An approving trill floated to them from a clearing on their left—a long, high-pitched whirring that sounded like a spaceship from an old science fiction film.

"American toad," a young man whispered beside Carolyn. "He's late for breeding."

The group marched on, unlit.

Carolyn paused by a large cedar and fumbled for her brochure. She squinted at it without light, then carefully cupped a hand around her flashlight so she could read about toads. Her hands glowed like a pink lantern under the evergreen.

Frank stopped with her and watched her frowning into the brochure. It was the same frown she had given her smudged canvas in the painting class she had taken last fall. Frank had dutifully taken the class with her, to support her efforts at self-improvement. When the frown deepened to a scowl, and Carolyn admitted defeat with watercolors, they both quit the class. Next for Carolyn there had been a quilting circle, which Frank had not joined. That lasted several weeks, until his sister discovered her backstitch was ragged and jaunty next to the even, tight lines sewn by the other quilters. She had showed Frank a sample swatch, the same rumpled frown pulling her features together like a dried plum. He followed the differing stitches with two fat fingers and offered to help his sister unpick her work. Now Carolyn was learning about Nature, so Frank was learning about Nature.

The title of tonight's lecture-walk, "Know Your Frogs," was backlit in flat block letters. The brochure also glowed in Carolyn's cupped light, and its creamy paper warmed his sister's face as she read.

"They breathe through their skin," she said, chewing her bottom lip.

The trail eventually began to run parallel to a pond that emptied into a thin, susurrating creek. The children in the group noted the pond first and whispered to each other that now, *now* they might see something. Ahead, the naturalist stood off the main path, one foot lowered into the reeds of the pond at the point where the trail came nearest the water. He raised his left hand to the group behind him, signaling for silence.

People grouped up slowly, edging toward him. Carolyn and Frank stood to his left in a half crouch. When the naturalist was satisfied he had enough followers around him, he turned his body sideways.

In the low tone of a priest blessing wafers, the naturalist nodded and said, "Eggs."

The gathered uttered a collective sigh, and the naturalist switched on his flashlight and eased its beam waterwards to a spot beside Carolyn. Behind a rock that protected a small, still corner of water from the expanse of the pond, a fine tangle of slimy rope looped under itself in a bundle near the reeds. The rope was clear and glistening, with black beads of movement inserted at regular intervals. It was as if some absent grandmother had dropped her mourning jewelry or an onyx rosary in the water, and now the strand was writhing, coming alive.

The pressure of the crowd behind her, all those people craning their necks and contorting to see the egg sacs, made Carolyn unsteady on her feet. In a thudding, excruciating moment, her left foot slipped awkwardly into the water. She teetered and fell, and her thick left leg landed sharply amid the delicate necklace of embryos.

The crowd gasped. Frank reached for his sister's arm and pulled her back quickly, firmly. She fumbled on her buttocks, then maneuvered her body into an awkward squat and finally stood. Frank held on to her as she tiptoed backward, away from the water. Her mortification was obvious; no one dared move.

Eventually an elderly female voice whispered, "Are you all right, dear?" and from somewhere in the darkness, someone offered another hand to steady her, a murmur of concern, a small towel. Ripples of water radiated out from where she had fallen, and here and there the splashes of creatures frightened off by the commotion broke the tense silence.

Carolyn nodded and shook her head, nodded again. She was unable to speak. She receded from the pond, back onto the trail, then across and off the trail again onto the other side, into the woods and up a small rise, finally coming to rest under a hemlock tree far from the group. Frank followed.

"Are you OK?"

Carolyn leaned her head back against the hemlock's trunk, nodded once, and said nothing.

"You sure, sissy?" Frank touched her shoulder.

Carolyn put a hand up, shook her head, then put the hand to her lips.

"It's all right," said Frank. "Frog eggs are tough. They'll be fine."

Carolyn exhaled heavily. The hemlock was sprouting some growth in the late spring. In the darkness, the light green of these new needles looked white, like snow on the tips of each branch.

"My knee hurts," she said finally.

In the distance, the naturalist dismissed the group briefly, and small subgroups formed along the banks, hoping to find more treasures. For the duration of this interlude, the naturalist kept to himself, off to the side of the pond.

"You sure you're OK?"

"Yeah." She pulled her voice tight to regain some dignity. "I'm going to rest my knee while everyone does this part." Carolyn looked up at Frank. "It's fine. Go look for frogs."

Frank dropped his hands from her and walked back toward the pond. The night air chilled him, and he recognized the deep *huuh* of a bullfrog as its call vibrated up from the water. In the dark, he followed it like a beacon.

A few minutes later, he felt guilty and looked back. He could just make out the pale outline of his sister. Carolyn was now standing on the trail, and the naturalist stood over her, his thinness in sharp contrast to Carolyn's round, vulnerable form. A stray flashlight wandered over them. The naturalist's eyes were black, his pupils fully dilated in the dark. His voice was low and cold, but Frank could not hear what he was saying.

Frank advanced, clenching his fists, but the naturalist had finished with Carolyn and walked away. She stood frozen and hunched in the dark.

"What did he say?" Frank asked when he closed the distance.

"Nothing."

"Was he being a dick?"

"No," said Carolyn. She raised her head and inhaled. "It's fine."

"Bullfrog!" shouted one of the children from the salamander family.

Several people shushed the child, but most scurried toward him with flashlights and thrilled, suppressed giggles. Carolyn watched the activity and joined the rear of the group. She did not giggle, but she walked with a determined gait Frank knew well enough. He followed.

The salamander boy was showing everyone a large male bullfrog resting on a rock jutting out of the water. Carolyn and Frank, the whole group, marveled at its lumpy ease, its huge eyes. As if to impress his audience, the bullfrog belted out a large, slow, belching croak that rattled the air around them. Frank felt the croak rumble across his shins, felt the vibrations on the undersides of his arms, at the edges of his eyes. They had all seen bullfrogs before, surely, but not like this. Not at night, in the deep, high wild. Not so big. Not so special.

"It can't see in front of itself," whispered the salamander boy. "They have a blind spot right in the front of their nose."

"Is that true?" someone asked.

No one answered. The gathered swarm leaned closer, trained more beams on their new celebrity.

The bullfrog licked its left eyeball. It lingered for a moment, bored or terrified, then eventually waddled away. Its front fingers grasped at the rocks and moss with deft, perfect certainty. Once he was gone, the group breathed together and mumbled approbation at what a fine specimen he'd been, what a loud, majestic croak he had. They had all seen him; the night was a success.

The naturalist loomed at the edge of all this activity. People uncrouched themselves and started back onto the path. Once they had reassembled, the naturalist made a brief speech about their fortune. He repeated some of his earlier statements about declining populations. "There are simply fewer specimens at this elevation now," he concluded, then waved his hand to move the group onward, back into the woods, away from the water.

"But what is happening?" asked a small woman with prematurely gray hair and muscular arms. "Why are they disappearing?"

The naturalist shrugged.

"Soil, perhaps. Frogs don't like acidity. We pollute. We rain it down. Acid gets in everything, even all the way up here. In the earth." The naturalist swooped one of his bat arms over the ground. "They leave; they stop breeding. It's difficult to say."

The little girl with the crooked braids started to cry. She had missed her chance to take a picture of the bullfrog, and she was concerned about the world ending and never getting to see another one. Someone, her father perhaps, tugged on her braids to console her.

The naturalist was off again. As everyone began to follow, Frank held on to Carolyn's elbow and maneuvered her past the group to the far side of the trail. He sat her down on a felled trunk and reached for her knee.

"Let me rub it," he said.

Carolyn did not respond. Frank stood both their flashlights on the ground in front of them, their beams shooting upward into the canopy and the night, so that for a little while, as they sat together alone, things did not seem so dark.

After a pause, Carolyn asked Frank, "Am I a good person?"

Frank was massaging his sister's knee in quick, awkward squeezes. "Of course you are. What in the world do you mean?"

"Nothing," said Carolyn. She pulled her leg slowly from Frank's hands. "Nothing."

"Why don't we go back," said Frank. "They'll be way ahead by now."

Carolyn sighed and allowed herself to follow Frank. He held both flashlights until they found their way to the group, then he handed one to Carolyn.

Back once again in the forest, away from the water, the naturalist was now standing with one foot on a large rock. Their group seemed smaller now, though Frank did not know whether that was right, or when or where they had lost members. He only noted the smell of ginger bug juice was not as strong as it had been before, and there seemed to be more air between everyone.

As Carolyn and Frank approached, the naturalist described the acreage of the station, how far the grounds stretched.

"It's not just this particular area. There are miles of national park all around us, in every direction. We work to keep everything hospitable, even for species we don't study. Sometimes the woods and the station seem as if they are all one. We have no fence. Crossover, cross-pollination."

He bent down to the boy who had found the bullfrog and salamander. "Lots of unwelcome visitors. Bumps in the night." The boy bent his knees, and his head shrank into his shoulders. Then the naturalist turned his back on the group and started to walk away.

"Are there . . . bears?" one of the other children asked.

"Oh, yes," the naturalist said without turning around. He waved his hand slowly in no specific direction, as if to indicate the ubiquitous presence of bears, the constant, unrelenting bearness of the place, and he glided into the black.

Carolyn huffed a sharp breath as she watched the naturalist recede.

"He keeps doing that," she whispered, mostly to herself.

"What?" asked Frank.

"He keeps *leaving* us," she said. "Some of us can't keep up with him. It's not right." She tightened her lips. "There are *children*."

Carolyn bent slightly and rubbed her knee. The rest of the group wandered after the naturalist, abiding his pull. The followers walked from a variety of directions toward him in a slow, inexorable creep.

Frank and Carolyn stood beside a large rhododendron bush just coming into bloom. Frank lingered there, staring at its fat buds and the round explosions of massive pink clusters holding themselves out, so brazenly, in the dark. He waved his hands around the flowers, along the waxy leaves, trying not to touch, touching. The petals felt like feathers against his palm.

Carolyn had carried on ahead. He caught up and soon found her at a wide spot in the trail. The starlight was brighter here, and the trail forked in a definite high- or low-road pattern. Just above them they could hear the rustle of the group on the high trail. Carolyn's moon-white legs, arms, her white T-shirted body, glowed before her brother. She was looking down a long, slow switchback that followed the left fork. All was quiet here.

"He said all the downward trails lead to the parking lot," she said, a new firmness in her voice. "Right?"

"Yeah," Frank said, "so I guess this other way is the right path." He nodded upwards, to the right and the dark figures gathered there.

"Well," said Carolyn. "I'm leaving."

Frank opened his mouth, but the back of his throat held tight.

He tried to make words but could only form his lips into a breathy "wh" sound.

"I'm done." Carolyn started down the sloping fork. "You stay if you want."

"But—" Frank managed, then stopped. He followed her, rustling up the muck of old leaves with his massive sneakers.

"It's fine, Frankie, if you want to stay."

"I thought you were having a good time."

"I'm not. I'm not at all. I don't like this, Frank. I don't like any of it anymore."

"Well, but . . ." He looked up to the high path again. "This was all your idea. What happened?"

"Him," said Carolyn. She wiped her eyes and jutted her chin behind Frank, toward the outline of the naturalist. Frank looked back. While the group continued walking, the naturalist had paused. He was crouching with his flashlight to peer at a lady slipper bud. His fingers were almost, almost touching it.

"I don't like where he's taking us, how he talks," she said. "And my knee hurts. I'm going back to the car."

Frank tilted his head, and in his best big-brother-by-four-minutes voice, he asked, "What did that man say to you?"

"He told me I was wearing the wrong shoes, and I should be careful. And he said something about the fragility of the ecosystem, or whatever."

"The wrong shoes," Frank repeated, smirking, and took a step back from her.

"Yeah. But it's the way he said it, and his whole . . ." Carolyn swooped her hand wide. "Just his whole thing with us. It's not right." She drew a breath to speak again, dismissed her thought. "He's not even *from* here."

"None of these people are. You and me are the only locals, I bet."

"Anyway. I'm going back to the car."

"But you said you wanted to learn about this stuff," he said.

"You're always talking about how we don't get outside enough, how we don't appreciate home."

Carolyn squinted and turned her body away from him. Frank reached out to touch her and grazed her arm with his hand. Her bicep felt clammy. Carolyn stared at her sandals. Her white toes wriggled like maggots in the gloom.

"Yeah," she said, "but I didn't think we were going to just, like, wander in it. I didn't know he was going to make us feel bad."

Frank cleared his throat. "Well, sissy," he replied, leaning into her, "this is nature. He's just showing us that. He's just telling us the truth about how we're not nice to it."

Carolyn's head snapped up. She peered at Frank, his round face, his beard. She glared at his hat, the sunglasses perched on its brim.

"I'm nicer to it than he is," she said.

A long silence followed.

"What does that mean?" asked Frank.

"I don't act like it belongs to me." She spun around and began to plod down the steep fork. "I'm going back. You stay if you want."

Frank stood in the wide patch of trail and watched her go. It would take her a while to find the car. There was time to visit another creek bed, maybe see a tree frog. He started upwards on the path. The group, now diminished to an even smaller band, was continuing deeper into the woods. Surely they would be circling back to the station and its buildings soon.

The naturalist stayed fully behind, at the back of the group for the first time, adopting a shepherd's position. The salamander boy and the girl with the braids were no longer visible. He kept his back to Frank, but there was a beckoning in the way his shoulders moved.

"On we go now," he called softly to the figures in front of him. His arms outstretched into the gloom, fingers splayed. "On we go."

Frank watched as the tiny band disappeared under a shadow of canopy. Late spring clouds were forming around the moon. It would be cold soon. Black. He wondered about the missing people and which trails they had taken in the night.

The naturalist stood surveying his remaining charges as they proceeded into the woods. He lowered his hands. Slowly, he turned around and caught sight of Frank. He paused as Frank moved toward him, up the path, away from Carolyn descending. The dark was getting deeper, and Frank could barely make out the naturalist's face. It seemed, for a moment at least, before he turned again and disappeared with the group, that he smiled.

Yes, that was it. The naturalist smiled, but not in a way Frank could be sure of.

DEVIL

"Being of these hills I cannot pass beyond."
—JAMES STILL

Tech Sergeant Boggs was beaten. He cracked his knuckles and stared out the windshield at the back streets of Cumberland. Sun seared through the glass onto his chest, and he rested an elbow on the open driver's window. He rubbed his right palm across the high sides of his fresh haircut—fast, back and forth, hot friction. The old man had stumbled upon him, and now Boggs had missed his chance to play things out his own way.

"Well." The low density of his father's baritone cut the air. "You planning to roast in there?"

When he arrived, Boggs had diverted the rental car into the parking lot of his old elementary school. He lingered and sweated for fifteen minutes. Before the old man showed up, Boggs had planned to hike up the last few blocks toward home. Slip onto their porch, ring the bell. Nod hello like it was nothing, keep the talk smooth and easy, a short visit to call things even in his mind. One night with the family, let them know what was happening, then up, out of these snaking hollers, and press on, mute and numb, until he landed in Bagram.

He stared up, above town, to the close stack of Kentucky mountains. The old man waited, a sliver of flesh at the lip of Boggs's side mirror. The hills loomed, deep emerald, over the six steep streets behind the elementary school. They skewed toward him, a rush of vegetation tilting from the peaks like a dark wave. The squat brick school to his right obstructed his view of town, with its boarded shop windows and broken bottles tossed along the edges of faded pavement. When he'd passed through Harlan twenty miles back, the rest of the world disappeared, and now, in his childhood hamlet, anything from outside, anything other, receded into implausibility. Boggs couldn't navigate past his view of the landscape leaning toward him, all of it one degree from toppling.

He pushed the butt of his palm against his brow, then reached into the backseat to heave over his dark-blue duffel bag. He popped the door latch and put a foot out onto fractured blacktop. He sighed and leaned out of the car, craning his head back toward his daddy.

Six four, sharp white button-down even on a Saturday, and mean as fuck. In his left hand, the old man gripped a plastic half-gallon jug purchased from the convenience store on the main road. He gripped it full, like a brick, not by the handle. The other hand swung loose, its meaty fingers tensing and releasing. The corded muscles in his wrist writhed. His glasses were cloudier than before, his pants too short. There was less of him than there had been the last time they'd seen each other. Still mean as fuck, though.

"Come on," his daddy said, flicking the jug. "Get on up to the house."

Boggs had told Cedarman he didn't want to come, didn't want to visit or even send a letter. But some hot piece of metal inside him, some charred grit, wouldn't rest until he'd done it. Cedarman, also a tech sergeant like him, told him everybody's got some shit they have to eat and wished him luck. Boggs's back still felt cool where Cedarman had touched him on the shoulder. He hoped he would be there when he shipped out.

Boggs swung the car door wide and hauled himself out. He

stood, just shy of six two, and held his duffel low at his side. He looked for as long as he dared at the school, studied the WPA cornerstone plaque and the heavy wood door. Then he squinted one eye back at his daddy. The late afternoon sun slapped his scalp.

"How long you been standing there eyeing me?"

"Long enough for my buttermilk to get warm." His daddy chucked his chin and turned, started the walk up home. He expected to be followed.

Boggs's mother was on the porch fanning herself and listening to the radio. He could see her from the end of the road, her face glowing haintlike at the far corner of the block. He slowed his pace and took in the street of his boyhood. Crackerbox shacks and tidy, square bungalows alternated down a narrow lane that seemed to drop off into an infinity of mountains, always green mountains. Everybody's house had a fence, some rattier than others. Almost everybody had a dog. From a few porches, flags hung limp in the heat.

As he advanced, his mother rose from a plastic deck chair and put down her funeral fan. She pinched the seams of her brown polyester dress and billowed it out, pulling the sticking fabric off herself. She watched the two men approach and bent her knees in recognition. Her body reminded Boggs of the hills around here in winter. Her arms flapped, and she grabbed her short, half-gray curls with one hand.

"Law, it's you."

She stepped out the screened porch door and into the tiny front yard. As Boggs closed the distance, she eyed him with a prim smile and reached out over the fence, clapping his biceps in a tight squeeze.

"You come up to see your momma." She stressed the last word with a girlish pitch.

"Yes, ma'am," said Boggs. He kept his eyes pointed at the ground and kicked the cracked concrete steps leading off the street into the yard.

His mother opened the wire fence gate for the two men and stepped back to let them pass. She hitched her hands onto her hips and watched her son.

"Well now," she said.

Boggs clomped onto the porch and followed his daddy into the house.

"Curtis," he heard his mother say, "why didn't you tell me you were going to get him?"

"Didn't know I was," said his father.

Boggs walked through the front door and a gust of A/C sucked the heat off him. The house smelled the same as always—a thick blend of pepper, mildew, and warm corn. The orderly living room was paneled in dark wood; the furniture hadn't changed. His mother watched him closely as he moved through, passed the front bedroom—his parents' room—on the right, and walked down the short hallway. He stopped just shy of the kitchen and turned left into his old bedroom.

It would have been a stretch to measure the room ten by eight. A small white desk sat under the window, cluttered now with his father's Bibles and cuttings from old magazines. On the single bed to his right lay a faded tartan blanket. Boggs dropped his duffel onto it and stretched his neck. He closed his eyes and listened to his mother begin to work in the kitchen. Now and then she said his name; she poked her head in twice.

On a high shelf above the bed sat a short stack of books, three framed pictures, and a rusty old cookie tin. Boggs swooped his arm in a layup and grabbed the tin as he lifted his feet off the floor. His body flopped on the bed with a dull whump, tin in hand.

He rifled through the unruly batch of cards and souvenirs inside. He had seen none of it since his last visit in '97, five years ago. He felt no flood of sentiment, or even much memory, upon touching each piece. He shoved everything back in the tin, stood, replaced it on the shelf, and stared out the window.

The stack of sun-bleached Bibles on the desk—King James, NIV, some in strange, glyphic languages—faded into a scatter of the old man's papers and clippings. The clippings got smaller as they reached toward the window. On the sill there were only fragments and remnants, some only a single word lying in the dust. A beige plastic window blind sliced the green outside into strips, and Boggs reached across the desk to pry open two slats. He still couldn't see anything except the same old wall of hills.

"Supper's on," his father announced from the doorway. Boggs turned, flexed his shoulders. The old man nodded at the duffel on the bed. "You staying?"

"Just tonight," he replied. "Have to leave tomorrow to get down to Cherry Point."

His father lowered his brow. "That's a marine outfit, ain't it?"

"Yessir."

"No sense for them to send you there."

Boggs nodded. "The other branches use it sometimes as, uh . . . as an exit point?" His voice lilted, quivered slightly.

The old man smoothed his hands down the legs of his trousers. "Is that for you to be moving on to somewhere?"

"Sir," the tech sergeant said.

He reached out and gripped his son's shoulder. At first the fierceness of the grip stunned Boggs into old fears, but his daddy hadn't moved to strike. They stood in silence.

It was a long time before he said with unfamiliar gentleness, "Son, let's go on in the kitchen. Tell your mother about it." He blinked, tightened his fingers in his son's shoulder.

They turned into the kitchen and took their usual seats at the table in the middle of the room. His parents had painted since his last visit; the cabinets were cream instead of wood, and a new border of yellow gingham paper ringed the top foot of wall below the dingy ceiling.

"There's cheese and crackers," his mother said into a pot on the stove. "Beans are almost ready."

"You been working on the place," he replied.

His mother looked around and waved a general assent at the gingham border. The family passed ten minutes in old rhythms. Bowls and utensils were set out, a fuss made over extra napkins. The old man poured each of them a glass of buttermilk, which Boggs never drank.

As he prepared to join his family at the table, the old man hitched his belt to adjust his pants. Boggs flinched, and his arms tightened against his chest. He stared at the plain gold buckle. His skin had known the lash of belt leather since toddlerhood, and the buckle stung a memory of teenage dander brutally quelled. His daddy cleared his throat and sat down.

They began their meal with a long prayer. The old man spoke of sin and unworthiness, noting his son's presence only indirectly. Per his usual, he invoked brimstone upon enemies, implored the heavenly father to protect this land, and blessed briefly any sacrificed souls. It had never been their custom to hold hands during grace, but Boggs's mother grabbed his fingers this time, then patted them after the amen. He twitched throughout. Her skin was cold and smooth, like always.

"Pastor Rick's saying there'll be another war," his mother said. She pushed the cornbread toward him. "Been talking about it every Sunday. About them Muslims."

Boggs did not reply.

"Will you have to go over there?" Her voice was loose, like she was pretending she didn't know or hadn't heard them in the other room before.

He chewed a spoonful of beans. The old man cleared his throat.

"Afghanistan," said Boggs finally.

His daddy's face didn't change, but his mother let out a low whistle and deflated inside her dress. Boggs mused on what Pastor Rick must have told them—accounts of black magic and swarthy demons riding the dusty hillsides of some foreign hellscape. His mother would chink extra quarters into the collection plate to hear these tales.

"You know where that is?" he asked her. She narrowed her eyes, nodded.

"We read about it," said his father. "We're always reading, son." He arced his spoon with curt authority toward a Lexington newspaper on the counter. A headline about President Bush denouncing Saddam appeared below the fold. "When do you go?"

"Two weeks."

"And you'll be doing what, exactly?"

Boggs shrugged. "Logistics, mostly. Maintenance. Ops checks," he said.

"Well, you're no soldier, I know that." The old man adjusted the paper napkin on his leg.

Boggs knew he'd meant it as comfort to his mother, but the comment stung him. "No shit, Dad. I'm Air Force."

His father's jaw twitched at the cuss spoken at his table, and Boggs felt a dull gladness fill his throat. He swallowed the power of the word.

"Fighting's grunt work," Boggs continued. "Marines. Army. Kids who can't think worth shit. They do the shooting, not me. I'm not putting my ass on the line for anybody."

His mother stared at him.

"I fix airplanes," he said to her. He rested an elbow on the table and tore at a piece of cornbread.

"So you'll be on a base," the old man said. "You won't be out there with the—" He glanced at the newspaper and seemed to pull a term from it. "Advance teams. You won't have a weapon." He gripped his glass, swung it to his lips, and held it there.

Boggs met his daddy's eyes. He savored the idea of telling them he'd be toughing it out in some movie-style operation, even though he would indeed be on a base, pushing papers and counting gaskets. His father had never served, never left Kentucky that Boggs knew of.

They held each other's gaze until his mother erupted beside them. Boggs watched as she wiped her eyes, but he could not see tears.

"Jesus, lord," she said, squinting hard. She rocked in her chair, pulled her hands down to clutch her neck, and was still.

They proceeded to eat in near silence, though there was some half-hearted talk of cousins and uncles. As they scraped the bottoms of their dishes, Boggs declined invitations to attend church or visit with anyone else before he left.

"I need to get on in the morning. Supposed to check in with medical, store some things."

His mother's lips disappeared at his refusal. When he tried to get up from the table, she shooed him back.

"There's that divinity," she said.

She walked to the fridge and fumbled around inside, eventually producing an electric pink and yellow divinity salad in a Tupperware bowl. As she muttered to herself, he noticed how thick her accent was; she came from deeper country than this place. He had forgotten how many sounds she packed into her words. She could lay four tight commands on him with a syllable. He thought of the round, calm enunciations of the men he worked with—scrubbed NCOs, officers with parchment degrees behind frames. All of them came from somewhere rich and plain. They spoke every letter, but still Boggs often missed their hints and jokes.

Back in high school, when he was looking to enlist, he had mumbled along with a navy recruiter, but Boggs was secretly afraid of water, so he hesitated signing up. Eventually, after he graduated, he visited some family down south, and his cousin's wife took him onto an air force base in Louisiana. Gears clicked in Boggs's brain when he saw the place. As they passed through the gate, he was reminded of the lofty cities he'd seen in old sci-fi pictures. Personnel bustled around meaningfully, without the sinister, egotistical energy of the grunts he'd seen elsewhere. He liked the way everybody was dressed, too. In the other branches, men only wore nice colors for important events, but the air force was all crisp blues. Sky-blue shirts, soft and inviting. And sleek jackets of an unfamiliar hue, somewhere between azure and navy, a color he wrongly identified as indigo. It was a fine, clean color. Even the mechanics looked like they had snap. No jeeps tooted around, either. Just sleek black autos and bona fide airplanes.

When they left through the back gate, his cousin's wife asked what he'd thought. Boggs said he thought everybody in the air force must sure be rich. That made her laugh. His cousin's wife was a captain. She had even spent time in Europe. Boggs joined at nineteen thinking he'd do six years in the same long, slow peacetime she'd enjoyed. He figured he'd escape Kentucky for the world, keep dirt and heat and fear at bay, safe in all that indigo.

A year later he was hosing off bombers in Desert Storm. The experience, everything about that detail vibrated inside him, like the muscle memory in his forearms after mowing a big lawn. He could scarcely remember speaking to anyone the entire year.

After '91, they put him on temporary duty at Wurtsmith to help shut it down, then a couple more flight lines, all over the map, for three-year stints after he reenlisted. Most recently, they had stationed him at Minot, North Dakota. There Boggs learned how to document his knowledge of jet engines and train other technicians. Minot was where he met Cedarman.

The first time he saw Cedarman, Boggs thought the man was a doll or an old church painting. The tech sergeant was indigo and smooth corners. Clean. Everything that had drawn Boggs to the service. Nothing, no cloud or dark mountain or heat, hung over Cedarman. He seemed totally unencumbered.

Cedarman was training to be an engineer, taking college classes in his off hours. When he checked out his tools every morning, he rubbed and studied each one until they were impossibly polished, and they stayed that way for him, no matter how dusty their work got. Cedarman supervised a small team of avionics technicians, senior airmen, and staff sergeants, the future tech sergeant Boggs among them. His job, he said, was to upgrade their tinkering skills to something the air force could use and to get himself promoted to master sergeant as fast as possible.

Cedarman and Boggs talked over and over about how the wires inside a cockpit were nerves driving the bird's reactions. Everything connected; solutions might be complicated, but the problems were always simple. Boggs was taller, Cedarman a few years older. Cedarman sometimes spoke to his chest or shoulders. Neither of them seemed to mind.

At Minot, the work was delicate and held his interest. Boggs was afraid of heights and had no aspirations to be a pilot. But Cedarman's explanations made sense to him, and he liked the idea of checking and rechecking a machine, putting it in the air, seeing the plane conquer the earth without having to go up there himself. It was enough that he could get something off the ground.

The other enlisted men at Minot complained of boredom, but Boggs liked the quiet, liked the detail. More than anything, he liked the flatness. North Dakota felt safe. He could see what was coming at him, everything out in the open. When he was off duty, he sometimes drove for hours, picking a direction and timing himself to see how far away he could keep the horizon, and for how long.

There were no fights or crashes at Minot. The weather was never a surprise, either, even when storms blew in. He could watch rain or snow tumble from afar and pass over him. Boggs widened his shoulders to this predictability. He breathed easy in the vastness. In winter, the whiteness of the plains in the snow reminded him of fresh paper and new bedsheets.

He did a good job at Minot, and Cedarman helped him get promoted from staff sergeant. Tech sergeants did less grimy work, which was a good thing at the right time, it turned out. When the twin towers fell, the whole unit was rushed to a huge base in Florida for eventual deployment to Bagram. Afghanistan meant working amid sirens and sleepless terror. At his current rank, Boggs would, at least, be inside a hangar when the bombs fell.

Next week, they would be corralled at Cherry Point before their maintenance squadron rejoined the air expeditionary wing. No one knew how long they'd be there or what Afghanistan would be like. He wondered how the planes would look flying over the Himalayas, if the mountains would scowl at him there the way they did here in Kentucky. He hoped someone there would keep him company, keep him from detaching his body from his brain again the way he had in Desert Storm.

Whether he loved Cedarman or whether he felt something like love for him was a problem Boggs hadn't yet worked out. He seemed like neither partner nor friend, but like an extension of Boggs's own body, a finer limb that had long ago come unglued from his own torso. He did not know how to make meaning from that. Cedarman, whose deployment orders were still pending, remained a tangle of warm wires. Though everyone in his outfit seemed to have decided he and Cedarman did indeed love each other, nobody asked or told. Their comrades left them alone, and the two men consulted no one—especially not each other. There was loveliness in the way Cedarman looked at him, and often impatience. But Boggs had never learned to extract or refine lovely things, and anyway, he was leaving. So he stilled and hushed and left the wires alone, raw and pure, inside himself. To preserve them, he reasoned, for later, when he was back in an open space with a longer, clearer view.

The Tupperware dish appeared on the table in front of him, and Boggs's mother doled out two glops of divinity salad for him and his father.

"Miss Judy's," she said.

Boggs noted the name; Miss Judy had been his teacher down at the school once. She had ratted him out to his daddy a number of times for fidgeting in class or tussling with other children, and she had been the catalyst for a string of harsh beatings when he was nine. She made pretty good desserts.

His mother turned to the counter and began cubing meat for a stew she was taking to church. His father sat with him at the table, reading the paper and ignoring Miss Judy's treat. The slop in the old man's bowl sat idle and sweated beads of fragrant pineapple water. Boggs ate slowly, sucking each chalky marshmallow one at a time. The sweetness hurt his teeth, and he wished for a cup of coffee to cut the flavor. His father finished reading and folded the newspaper neatly. He raised his spoon in one hand and stared into the divinity.

"This war," he said as he tapped the newsprint with a middle finger, "will be long." His spoon clinked in his bowl. "On that point I disagree with your Mr. Rumsfeld."

"He ain't mine," said Boggs. "Hell."

"They're saying we'll go to Iraq next." The old man pronounced it "eye-rack," which made his son's mouth twitch. "A place you'll know."

Boggs thought back to his brief experience in the Gulf twelve years before. He had barely been an airman then, doing little more than gawping at F-15s. He had actually been stationed in Saudi Arabia, not Iraq, but it didn't matter; he never left the base. He rarely even left barracks if he wasn't on duty. The heat unnerved him, much as it had his whole life, but the desert was worse than Kentucky summers. The sun burned huge and malignant; it cracked the paint off planes, pulled sand around the way the moon pulls tides. Boggs shut his brain down in that heat and stayed mentally absent for days, weeks at a time.

"I don't know much about Iraq"—he took care to pronounce it "ee-rock"—"except I don't want to go."

"Ancient land," said his father. "Eden." His mother continued chopping meat with her back to them, but they could both tell she was listening. "Place is full of struggle."

Boggs wanted to laugh or cough or interrupt. He wanted to break the meniscus his father always pulled over a room. When the old man spoke to anyone too long, they'd shift sideways, one foot creeping out from the film of dread around him, waiting to escape. He was just a postman, but everybody in town feared his daddy. The house rarely had visitors.

Boggs could think of nothing to say; it didn't seem worth explaining that Iraq was a whole other war that hadn't even started yet. There would be no convincing his father of simple geography when he was pondering some larger notion. The hard light in the kitchen stunned his wits. Evening gloomed outside.

"Don't turn from your duty," his father said. "The Lord judges our fight against godlessness. We must finish what we started there, in His name." He jabbed his spoon into the bowl a few times, shook his head. "Backwards place, the Middle East."

Boggs rolled his eyes up to the ceiling. The old, hot sludge that sloshed in him whenever his parents talked Religion began to ooze through his veins.

"Yeah?" he said. "Is that right."

He stuffed his hands in his pockets and rocked the chair onto its back legs. He chucked his head in the direction of the main road. "As opposed to the sanctified peace they got down there at the Piggly Wiggly? I don't see how Over There is any more backwards there than Right. Here." Boggs tapped his foot to mark the last two words.

"But you love backwards places, I guess." He pitched forward in his chair. "Anyway, long or short, I'll be there, not you."

He pulled his feet toward himself, and they made a papery sound on the worn linoleum. Pride swelled in his guts. Boggs was old enough, finally, to answer back.

"You don't know shit about it," he said to his father.

A shock cracked across Boggs's cheek. His head jerked to the left, then swung back with a snap. He turned into the pain and saw his mother standing over him, her jaw twisted sideways. She held a butcher knife above him and was arcing it in a grim follow-through. Its cheap steel glowed under the kitchen light. She had slapped him with the flat side of the blade.

His hand crept to his face to check for blood, his eyes fixed on her. The sting of the knife's tip was humming near his ear. Though there would be a welt when he left in the morning, his mother had not broken skin.

"You quit your sass and mind your daddy," she said. Her eyes were like brackish water. "You been hateful and sassing since you got here."

Boggs turned his head from her and rubbed his cheek again. He pushed back against the smallness coming over him. He tightened his arms against his rib cage for ballast.

"Momma, I'm thirty-two."

It was all he could think to say. He checked himself for blood once more, rubbed his hand on his gray T-shirt. "Goddamn."

"Don't." She raised the knife in a quick fist, and her son flinched. She lowered her hand and turned back to cutting meat.

Across the table, his father had bowed his head and risen from his chair.

"Son," he said slowly, "you've got the devil in you."

A cold tingle rippled across Boggs's hairline. The kitchen walls bowed and distorted around him, like he was stuck inside a convex mirror. He panicked now because he didn't know what time it was. He might have to suffocate like this for hours, until he could go, until he could get out, away from them, and he didn't know how to count those hours.

Boggs tensed his neck around his voice box to tamp down any shake or squeak. "The hell kind of holy roller shit are you talking now?"

His father spoke over him and cut off the end of his question. His voice was hard, but he did not stir or shout. His body was rigid.

"It's a devil that's got you. Always has. You've had a wickedness since you were a boy."

His mother grunted agreement.

"Disrespectful," she said. "Always hiding in there. Strange." She poked her knife toward his tiny room. "Didn't even have a kiss for his momma when he walked up. Just as stubborn and strange . . ."

His father shut his eyelids, which were paper-thin and mazed with purple lines.

"I pray the discipline of your service casts out the darkness in you and brings you to the light of the savior. I pray for that every night."

Boggs stood. He crumpled his paper napkin in his fist and drew himself up to his full height. Whatever happened in Afghanistan, whatever he hated or feared there, would still cost less than this. He had no reply, so he cursed again.

"Goddamn. Hell with it," he said, and turned to leave.

A sharp thud shattered the gloom. Boggs froze. The table rattled as his father slammed his hands down two more times. The old man's palms were stretched out, and the veins of his forearms popped livid. The house vibrated with his blows. The static in the air cut against Boggs's skin, made it itch.

His mother cowered by the stove. The old man gripped the back of his chair and swung his head toward his wife. Soft, softer than he usually said things, his father said, "Lost."

His daddy leaned back toward his son.

"He's been lost to us a long time, Mother."

His daddy swayed over the chair. He appeared ageless now, unchanged, just as he had been in Boggs's boyhood. Out the back window of the kitchen hung the hills, close, unrelenting, bringing on night, early and black.

Boggs exhaled and longed for cooler air in his lungs. He gritted his teeth and thought of Cedarman—his uniform, his clean tools and careful speech. The vast, snowy plains of North Dakota, then its broad sky, appeared to him, and at long last, he found the word that described how he had always felt there: *revealed*. Heaven, Boggs decided, must be a wide, quiet pasture of fine and perfect snow.

Boggs wished he could fight the old man, just once. Break off a chair slat and lay into him until he whimpered for mercy. He knew he could do it, mentally at least. But there was no telling how much gristle his daddy kept in reserve. His father could probably still beat him senseless, perhaps even crack his son's ribs as he had done once twenty years ago. He would need no weapon. The old man's hands were hard enough on their own, like planks of ash.

"Fine then," said Boggs, putting up his hands. "Fine. I'm licked. I own it."

His mother shook pepper into her stew.

The old man stared at his shoes and cupped the top spindles of the chair with his palms.

"I'll be out of your hair in the morning," said Boggs. "First light."

He waited for a response, but none came.

"I ain't coming back. You hear? You done run the devil out of town."

He pointed at the door to his room. "And I don't want those pictures or nothing in there. You can burn all of it. Bunch of junk."

He backed himself down the hall, swaying his shoulders in broad arcs as he receded. The rusting refrigerator switched itself on as he passed it, and a thrum fluttered through the kitchen. His parents' movements loosened at the familiar noise of the appliance. His mother continued cooking, and his father eased himself back into his chair and picked up his divinity bowl.

Boggs backed fully into his bedroom. He closed the door, leaned a hand against the frame for a moment, then sat down on the bed. Night finished coming on as he dug out a few supplies from his luggage and plotted the long drive to Cherry Point. His hands fumbled with his road map and pencil, and blood roared in his ears until he gave up. He turned off the tiny table lamp and lay down on his side, on top of the tartan bed cover. He had not bothered to undress; he didn't want to fight the trembling in his hands.

Eyes open in the shadows, Boggs imagined the cool interior of the waiting airbus that would soon take him away, along with scores of other men from his squadron, and men in thousands. He wondered if he'd ever get back to Minot, and whether Cedarman's orders had come in yet. Then Boggs pulled his duffel into himself, embraced its indigo canvas with both arms, and broke. His body slackened, his feet curled under him in the darkness, and he broke like a child.

QUEEN

On her memory, the hive sat in the side yard, echoing family rituals and routines. Summer mornings, workers would swarm the basil plant on the porch. They bothered no one—not even Dale, whose deck chair always sat close by.

Maisy could scarcely think of a time she had been stung on her mother's property. So familiar were the movements and flight paths of all participants that it never occurred to anyone to disturb each other. The spread of acres kept them all satisfied to go their own way, and making room for others rarely interrupted anyone's foraging. So when Dale texted her about the half-empty hive and the carnage littering the hydrangea bushes, Maisy left work early, pulled her hair up into a ponytail, and barreled down Highway 23 to her mother's house.

She arrived to find Dale upright and between beers. His face was puffy as usual, his skin splotched red and brown from six decades of abandoned anger. He nodded gently and tugged his baseball cap as Maisy pulled up, then went back to working on the lawn.

"Are they all dead?" she called out as she slammed her car door. Maisy edged toward Dale, but she made sure to stay close to the house. She didn't want to look for herself. "Where's the queen?"

Dale shrugged, killed the weed whacker, and staked it into the ground like a ski pole. He didn't know anything about bees. Dale hadn't been around yet when they brought the hive home years before, and it was one of the few things he didn't look after here. He said he didn't like to mess with a body that didn't mess with him. In return, the bees left him alone when he dozed near their favorite spot on the porch. Dale's drunken fogs were protracted, but largely harmless. The bees seemed to respect, even admire, the depth of his hazes.

She asked after her mother, and Dale shrugged again, this time with more resolve.

"She's still in that damn jar, Maisy," he muttered, "right where you left her." He spat into the grass and sighed heavily through his nose.

"All right," she said. "Let me go see what I can figure out."

Dale looked out toward the road and rubbed the dirt from his hands onto his T-shirt. His fingers were thick and calloused. "What the hell," he said as Maisy eased past him. "I'm not gonna scatter her in the bushes. You want her, take it home with you."

She squinted hard, reminded herself to be patient, and trudged up to the house. For all ten years they were together, Dale had made breakfast for Maisy's mother every morning. When the cancer took her appetite, he brought her green tea instead and waited patiently as she agonized over each sip, all the while aching to get downstairs and have his own first drink of the day. Through it all, and even now after her mother's passing, Dale still kept the lawn mowed, still fixed the pipes when they dripped. He knew it wasn't his house, so Maisy let him stay on for now. It was easier than keeping up two houses by herself. She figured he'd move out soon, maybe go live with his ex-wife in Sevierville. In the meantime, she tried to remind herself she would be lucky to find a man so devoted, drink or no drink, someday when her own children left her.

She paused on the porch to move Dale's cooler off the top step, then went inside to find the apiary handbook.

Maisy didn't know anything about bees, either, not really. What little she remembered she had learned only by watching her mother, who rarely talked of how or why with any of her garden work. Even those few scraps of knowing were long distant acquisitions, all earned over a decade ago. When her kids were still little, Maisy had moved back home for a year. She finished her GED, then her accounting certificate, riding out the ravages of her divorce and pushing back against whoever tried to stop her. She moved out again as soon as she could afford to, but her mother still liked to tell people Maisy grew up in this house—twice. She gritted her teeth whenever her mother said things like that. All her mother's friends thought Maisy had a square jaw.

The bees had arrived during that year Maisy and the kids lived with her mother. Ever since then, the bees had been part of the landscape. Maisy knew just enough now to suspect the hive was dying. There was nothing to be done, but she hunted in the kitchen cabinets for the book just the same.

***

"I want to get some bees," her mother had said to her. She cuddled Baby Girl in her arms; they were making faces and giggling at each other.

"Momma," Maisy replied, waving at the paper wasps idling under the side porch, "you've already got plenty."

"You know what I'm talking about," she said from the side of her mouth. Hunter ran past them, aiming his water pistol at his old tricycle. Her mother touched Hunter's skinny shoulder as he doubled back to growl a militaristic oath at one of his other toys.

"I didn't do it when you were little," she said as Hunter disappeared behind the house. "You were always getting into a mess.

Didn't want to listen." Maisy tightened her lips as her mother bounced Baby Girl a time or two. "But these two . . . My grandchildren need to make some honey."

And so they drove out to Murphy. She knew an organic farmer whose uncle raised bees way out there, just shy of the state line. "Good bees," her mother said. "No chemicals. He's got them so they don't give a damn about anything but making comb."

How the woman knew this, Maisy never thought to ask. They borrowed June's new truck and drove down 74, following the map her mother had drawn on the back of last month's propane bill. June lived next door; she and Maisy's mother had known each other decades, husbands, bodies ago. They talked together like old thieves almost every day and even wore their hair in the same long, gray braids.

Maisy didn't remember how long they all stayed there or what prices or logistics were negotiated for buying and transporting the hive. That memory was a dozen years old. Perhaps she was told to sit on the porch with her children while the business was conducted, but she preferred to think she chose to do so.

"You keep the queen, Maisy," her mother said. "But for heaven's sake, be careful with it."

She handed over a little cardboard jewelry box and marched back to the truck. Maisy's mother's arms stretched down like old wires. They hung from her like afterthoughts while she plowed on to wherever she was headed. That's how Maisy remembered it: a long arm depositing the queen with her from a distance, then whizzing past. Maisy fumbled with the box, stuffed it deep in the pocket of her favorite hoodie, and trudged along behind.

On the ride home, her mother drove and chatted, mostly to herself. The hive sat in the bed of the truck, and Hunter and Baby Girl napped on the tiny backseat in the cab. The engine revved all the way back up the mountain while her mother went on and on.

"No chemicals, the man said. I'll just use a little menthol and thyme when I need to." She looked in the rearview mirror at Maisy's kids. "We'll smoke them out when they're good and ready," she chirped, "and have us a little treat for those grandbabies soon."

Maisy looked out the window and watched the mountains darken around her. She felt small, like she could fit into the backseat with her children, and she could think only of the queen in her hand. Rarely were such important items entrusted to her. She wanted to look at the queen so badly, to study it while it was alone, away from the colony, but she didn't. Her mother would kill her if it flew away, so Maisy kept her hand inside her pocket, holding the box close to her. The whole thing felt like it mattered somehow, so for all the things she forgot, she remembered that part.

Her mother dithered and fretted over the hive for a few days, and then it was like they had always been there. Maisy's kids never feared the bees or ran from them. They were just always around, hovering and tending to their own concerns. "They sure have settled right in, haven't they?" her mother beamed one morning as she watched a fat worker stagger out of a peony.

***

A few months later, after the weather started staying hot even into the early morning, her mother called June over from next door, and the two women worked out a plan for harvesting the honey. They had no centrifuge or fancy equipment, so instead they drank scuppernong wine and remembered their childhoods until they settled on the best method they knew. June had a mask and an ancient smoker, so they fetched those and told Maisy to keep the children inside, inside no matter what. Maisy had no idea what they were doing out there; she could only see so much from the house.

Soon the kitchen came alive with giggles and movement. Her mother put a huge sieve and a clean plastic bucket in the sink. She grabbed some kind of putty knife and told Hunter to help her scrape the comb off the frames. Hunter quickly took to being trusted with such a grown-up-looking job, and soon the sieve was overflowing as the honey drained into the bucket.

"Now," her mother said to her son and Baby Girl with great portent, "now, we squish!"

The children took turns squeezing the comb and squealing. Maisy took over when Baby Girl tried to put her head in the bucket. The warm ooze of wax and honey on Maisy's hands felt like some old, fine thing she knew well, even though her mother had never allowed her such pleasures when she was little. She continued to squish, dimly registering June's reminders to save the beeswax for her.

When Maisy turned from the bucket to wipe her hands, she saw her mother handing down a bit of comb to Baby Girl. The toddler stood, wide-eyed and enraptured, one hand almost entirely in her mouth while the other hand reached up, the rest of her as still as earth, for that scrap of sweet. Every inch of Baby Girl was covered in honey. In her hair, down her back, between her toes—it was as if she had rolled in the stuff. June laughed and hooted as she leaned against the doorframe, egging everyone on. Maisy could only think of getting both children into the bathtub as quickly as possible.

All told, the sticky chaos of their first harvest yielded barely a gallon. The following year, her mother and June refined their technique. The honey came just after Maisy moved with the kids into a new duplex in Waynesville. Maisy liked her job, and the children could go to a good school, one with computer labs and a real football team. Her mother dropped off four big jars as a housewarming gift, and for months the kids insisted on putting "goo"—butter and honey stirred together—on their toast every morning.

Dale showed up a little while later. He built a new shed, made her mother laugh, and settled into the deck chair on the porch. The bees continued as ever. For the next few summers, Hunter would ask to go over the mountain and help his grandmother with the hive. Maisy usually just dropped him off. His first year at Haywood

Middle, Hunter went to Vacation Bible School camp and missed the honey harvest. After that, the bees rarely caught his attention. When he made the high school varsity football team and had to practice through the summers, he stopped visiting his grandmother's house altogether. All he wanted was a football scholarship, a ticket out of town.

***

Last year, right after her mother's diagnosis, Hunter packed off to college in Georgia, and two of June's four hives died. The frames came up empty, light as anything when she lifted them out. Maisy's mother comforted her old friend and offered her a jar from her own stores. She did not mention her illness. Maisy brought them both a glass of iced tea and sat down nearby to sort through a pile of doctor bills while they talked. June kept worrying aloud, her voice high pitched and endless.

"Oh, what is it, I wonder?" June keened. "What's making them leave the queen? Do they just . . . do they get lost?"

She kept staring out the kitchen windows, red-eyed, bobbing her graying head as if hoping to see a swarm of familiar faces. June wrapped her arms around herself inside a worn blue buttondown shirt that had belonged to some husband or another. Then she started quoting Shakespeare, something about sitting on the ground and telling sad stories about dead kings. Maisy had to chew her pencil to keep from getting up and swatting her.

"There, now," her mother had said. "I'm sure none of it's your doing, honey."

***

This year, in all the bother and confusion of watching her mother die, Maisy had forgotten to ask how June's remaining hives were faring. It was spring, and she had had bigger things on her mind. Taxes would soon be overdue on her mother's house, and no one could find the insurance policy for the car. The apiary guide had apparently disappeared, too. Besides, Dale said June hadn't been stopping by so often like she used to. Neither had Maisy, but Dale didn't say anything about that.

As Maisy rifled through the kitchen cabinets for the beekeeper's book, she glanced into the dining room at the pewter urn sitting on the mantel. Her face reddened. Maisy lowered her hands and looked away, out a window into the side yard.

"Momma," she whispered, "you've got to tell me where you keep things."

Maisy thought she'd better go up and check on her mother's room. Perhaps the book was there, and she could tidy up a little, water the plants. The upstairs hall was a long series of doors. All the bedrooms were tiny and hot; in the summer, half the doors swelled in the heat and sealed themselves shut.

On the stairs, a weight overtook her. Lately, Maisy had made it her job to check the progress of the seedlings on the bedroom sill during her visits. But she found today she was ready to let them go. Whether there were tomatoes to plant this year didn't matter. Dale would forget to tend them or accidentally mow them, and she had little time for canning even if they did survive until their fruit ripened. Maisy shook her head. Only six weeks since her mother's funeral, and already the whole house had been abandoned.

She rested her hand on the banister, smoothed it up and down slowly, and decided to leave things as they were. She needed to get home. Her daughter was supposed to cook a "traditional" family dinner this week and document the process for English class. So far the preparations had been disastrous, with Baby Girl huffing and brooding in a cloud of corn flour and angst.

She returned to the kitchen and puttered through the cabinets, hoping her son would come home from college for spring break. She paused in the breakfast nook and looked out the big window to watch Dale unlocking the shed. Maisy figured he kept working on the yard for the same reason she still changed the sheets on Hunter's bed every week. It was something to do, a muscle memory. Just like whenever Maisy drove to Asheville and got scared in all that traffic. With every near miss and honked horn, she'd reach her hand out to the empty seat beside her, just in case, to protect phantom children long gone from the passenger seat.

In between the panes as she looked out, Maisy spotted a shriveled drone pawing meekly at the glass. Her eyes focused on the sills and screens all along the big window. Scores of drunken, half-dead insects lay writhing alongside the curled husks of their comrades who had already succumbed. Maisy stared for a long while and wondered where the thousands of others had gone, whether they were sick, or dead, or just forgot where home was. She blinked and thought about the sound they used to make when all was in bloom.

Tomorrow, or maybe the next day, if she remembered to, she would ask June about her hives. If the rest of June's bees are dying, too, Maisy thought, if they've got the same sickness, well, I guess I'll take it as some kind of a sign.

Her phone vibrated in her pocket. She reached for it, read a text from her daughter. Barely looking at the keypad, Maisy let her fingers click and dance their reply: *Yes, Baby Girl. Forget cooking. I'll take us into town for supper.*

Outside, Dale fired up the lawn mower. The house filled with a low, angry buzz. Maisy glided through the house and out onto the porch, closed her eyes, and waited for the smell of fresh-cut grass to come to her. She hovered in that moment alone and familiar, and almost forgot her plans to leave.

MEAT

The receiving line snaked through the chapel, its center aisle a corpus of grief, clutched purses, dark jackets. Miss Florence had insisted on cremation and a rented casket, had made her nieces promise only minimal fuss, because why spend good money on old bones? But then everyone showed up to pay respect because they or their children had all spent time under Miss Florence's care at the early childhood center. After forty years of wiping noses, Miss Florence always liked to say, everyone in town was her baby. Even the pastor had been one of her babies, a long time ago.

The service had been packed, and now hundreds pressed together in the best of gluts, waiting to offer condolences to Miss Florence's family. It was early autumn, that hushed, forthright season, and the chapel hummed with good, clean, true grief.

Samuel Ammons brought his eldest granddaughter, Alison, who had not been one of Miss Florence's babies. Alison was only visiting, and she was not a churchgoer. She wore a borrowed dress, collared and polka-dotted, which aged her considerably. The dress clung to her back, and sweat dampened the dark curls on her neck. Alison looked feeble compared to everyone else—a mountain girl startled and shied by the flatland's October heat, the only unsmiling mourner.

"No, this is my *grand*daughter. This is Bryce's girl," Samuel said to the small knot of people around him in the receiving line. "Down from the hills." He touched his fingers to Alison's narrow shoulders. "We sure like having her visit with us. She's all grown now."

Everyone nearby in line nodded.

Well now, young lady, the mourners said, I expect you're in school.

"She's studying agriculture," said her grandfather.

Everyone approved. There were still farms in this town.

"Alison works in the university dairy," Samuel said. "Bet you didn't know App State owns that outfit over in Statesville? Milks a-hundred-sixty cows every morning, don't you, Alison?"

Alison's mouth felt sticky; she kept her lips shut and nodded. Everyone approved again.

The front of the church was cluttered with lilies, ribbon-bright bouquets, an ornate easel with a photograph of Miss Florence, mementos, the sleek casket. Someone had parked an ancient, rusty tricycle under the easel.

"They switched her out from the hog farm this summer," Samuel said. "She had to go back home a while to rest."

Oh, was it the heat? the mourners asked. You won't be used to that, they said. Poor thing.

People here did not think of the Blue Ridge Mountains as the South or of Alison as anything but a stranger. She came from a wet, unknowable labyrinth of hollers, and she had been confused by the order of hymns during the service. The mourners peered at her as if they were thinking of snow or of wildcats slinking low to the ground.

Samuel shook his head, lowered his voice. "She didn't like the slaughterhouse."

Everyone sighed. *Ah*. They wrinkled their noses compassionately. They knew the industrial hog facility just a few miles from here. They knew its smells, its lagoons of dung and chemical runoff that festered in the sun. They knew the cages, the livestock trucks rattling down the cracked county highway every day, each one packed with terrified, pink bodies.

Alison crossed her arms and dipped one hip toward the casket, which loomed nearer as the receiving line inched forward.

For a whole month, she had worked in the main hog farrowing barn. The barn was the largest of five metal tubes at the end of the facility. Its ceilings were thirty feet high, rounded. Metal. Metal walls, metal roof, metal gestation cages. Metal fans whirred constantly above, but the barn stayed hot. The air was thick with sweat and shit and the tang of aluminum and scalding summer humidity. Everything echoed and reeked.

She was the only student intern. For everyone else, the place was a job. So they gave Alison the worst duties: scraping muck and sludge, culling dead, filthy piglets from cages where they'd starved or been trampled.

The noise. The smell. Alison was small, and the workers joked she was so skinny she would slip through the gratings in the floor if she wasn't careful. The animals bit her. They screamed. Her skin cracked open in the heat. The hogs' skin cracked open in the heat. Sows clamored and writhed, sometimes six to a cage. Nothing was clean. Even the ceiling was coated in grime.

She had been glad, at first, when the place was destroyed.

"It's tough work," said Samuel. "Wasn't for her." He patted his belly. "So she went back up the mountain a while, finished up her credits. Tested out of a bunch of classes, didn't you?"

Alison nodded again, moved her tongue around to loosen the thick spittle in her mouth.

"Then they switched her to the dairy. Inspections, monitoring."

He chucked his chin toward her. "She knows all about milk and eggs now, don't you, honey?"

Is that right? said the people in line.

"She'll do all right for herself," said Samuel. "She could work for Jimmy Dean. She could work for Dairy Maid."

The air in the church was dense with flesh. So many people, good country people, a line of them ambling past the body, the pulpit, to Miss Florence's family, then out the church's side door, to the parking lot, to home, to their hot suppers elsewhere.

They moved like sows. Like animals. Alison had seen it. She had seen this same slow movement in milk cows on their way to be pumped, in heifers corralled for tagging and ewes heavy with mud-caked wool.

Her grandfather was wrong. Alison had not switched to dairy studies, but to crop science. Her dairy internship was only temporary, a two-week stint to make up the required hours she lost over the summer. And it had not been the slaughterhouse that made her change majors.

Her sows had burned.

The morning of the fire, she had arrived for work at seven thirty. She wore thrift store clothes—all her own T-shirts had acquired an eye-watering, unwashable funk after just one shift in the barn, or been badly torn, so at the end of each day, she trashed whatever she was wearing. Soon her suitcase, which sat in her grandparents' spare room, was empty. Her closet at home, full of white skirts and thick sweaters, felt far away, and she often wondered if she'd ever be clean enough to wear them again.

She turned into the hog facility's long gravel drive that morning and found the whole compound was strewn with fire engines. First responder trucks were parked haphazardly in the grass. The smell of charred filth seeped through the vents of her tiny car. She pulled over and parked by the maintenance trailer where workers went to collect their weekly paychecks. When she got out, the burned air stuck to her like some unseen tar. The roof of her mouth itched.

Someone called to her, "Hey runt!"

Alison sprinted up to a group of coworkers. They were walking toward the farrowing barns, the largest of which was gone. In its place was a black, smoking ruin. She asked what happened.

"Fire," they said. "Main barn caught fire last night."

How did it start?

"Electrical is what they told me," someone else said. "All them old wires caught light, then the timber framing, I guess. And the supply lofts. Would have been fast."

"It's almost out," said a woman who had laughed at Alison on her first day when she learned she was a college student. "They better let us help with the cleanup. I need my check."

It was hot. The morning sun was already a knife. Alison asked about the animals.

"Cooked," someone said, nodding at the barn. "They cooked in there."

"It's a mess," said the woman who had laughed at her. "I saw it happen one time when I worked for this big outfit down east. All that metal. Once a spark gets going, the whole thing's an oven."

As they walked toward the massive black hull, Alison almost went back to her car and drove home. Not home to her grandparents, but back home to the mountains, all the way up the interstate, through that channel of hills, to her parents' house, or better still to her dorm room on her hilly campus, to white skirts and thinner air. She wanted to quit, run away, but she still needed two hundred more internship hours to graduate.

Alison asked if they would be laid off.

A few people laughed. "There's four other barns," they told her. "Always plenty more hogs coming in, going out. Plenty of work, always."

Her supervisor approached the group and told them the fire

was mostly extinguished and that they should come back that afternoon to start the cleanup effort. His face looked gray.

Alison asked him, Is it bad?

"Come back after lunch," he said.

In the afternoon, the workers walked to the main barn together. All that metal, so much heat. Flesh. Hogs are just flesh, and they had indeed cooked, alive in the fire, through the night. As they approached, the scent of smoke and carnage made a wall Alison could almost lean into.

Someone handed her a dull pickax and walked into the barn. The great curved roof above them was warped and black, and parts of it had collapsed. The floor was lifeless chaos: ash, charred beams, mounds of black tissue, bloodied bone. Stillness. She closed her eyes and pictured the living barn, before the fire. A thousand pink ears twitching under those giant fans, the hogs' grunts and screams, her own body alive among them. She gripped the pickax and backed away.

It took six days to clean out the main barn. The workers shoveled and scraped, mostly without safety equipment. Rotating shifts gutted the place so a construction crew could later rebuild the timber framing, rewire everything. Alison did what she could, but after a few minutes' effort, even with a respirator, she would retch and have to go outside. Her supervisor finally put her on hosing duty.

"Just wash it down," he said, pointing to the concrete drive behind the barn and some machinery scattered around. "Wash everything down." There was a river nearby that could carry away almost anything.

They found the sow on the second day. No one knew what to do about her.

She was huge, alive, rustling under the grate. No one could figure out how she got there, how she'd survived the flames. Alison put down her hose and followed the crowd to investigate.

She peered down into the underfloor, the only part of the main barn that hadn't burned or been left in tatters. The underfloor was a crawl space below the grates, where all the piss and muck and death from above dropped down.

The sow was huge. The biggest Alison had ever seen. Her back was badly burned and cut open. The deep wounds looked like gashes from a whip.

They called the supervisor, who stared down at her and nodded.

"It happens," he said with a shrug. "She probably fell between some grates when she was a little piglet."

Alison asked how the sow could have lived.

"There's plenty to eat down there," he said. "Just catch what falls. No one to bother you. We only muck it out every couple of months." He cocked his head, sizing her up. "She's mature," he said, impressed. "Bet she's been down there a year."

Her supervisor continued staring at the sow. They all did.

"It's a good place to hide." He pointed vaguely east. "We'll have to open that side fence, over by the drainage pipe. Try to coax her out."

The sow grunted, sloshed a hoof in the black muck. Alison knelt down. Its eyes, she noted, looked like a child's. Round and aware.

"I guess she heard it all," he said. "Just stayed hid; found someplace wet and waited it out. She was smart."

It took six workers to extract the sow. After she was caught, the supervisor let them eat her.

One of the older workers, someone who knew how, slaughtered her so they could have a barbecue. Alison did not watch the slaughter. She knew it would be swift if not merciful, and she was grateful for his expertise. After the sow was bled out, the older worker and two helpers gingerly loaded her carcass into the back of his truck, then drove her to a meat locker on the other end of the facility, where she would hang for a few days to tenderize.

The barbecue was held to celebrate finishing the cleanup. They pit roasted the sow under a heavy black drum. The wafting smells brought every last worker out for the meal. All the supervisors came, plus the administrative assistants in the payroll trailer, and even a few of the first responders and firemen who had helped put out the blaze.

They ate her off Styrofoam plates, down by the river on the seventh day.

Alison ate only a cob of corn, nothing else. Gristle and marrow churned inside her. The next day she quit. She emailed her advisor, filled out the change-of-major forms online, and told her grandparents she wouldn't be back until the fall.

She carried it all summer, carried it still. The cleanup, the smells and screams, the whole experience of the hogs weighed on her, silenced her. Before this, she had had no idea.

"I'm so sorry," said Alison as she approached Miss Florence's family.

She moved down the funeral receiving line, where no one recognized her. Her grandfather kept a gentle hand in the middle of her back, piloting her toward the nieces of Miss Florence, who were huddled together against a white wall. People leaned over them, sighing, embracing, blocking their view. The nieces looked dazed and trapped.

Ahead, beyond the murmuring bodies, people took their leave and passed, one or two at a time, to the side door of the church, which led out to the parking lot. The exit flapped open, pierced Alison with hot afternoon light, then closed again. Flapped open, pierced with light, then closed.

"For your loss," Alison said, nodding at one of the nieces. "I'm sorry."

She moved along, nodded again.

"I didn't know her," she said. "Nice to meet you. I'm so sorry."

SAINT

Your brother is going to die in twelve years. It is winter. Lake Huron has frozen, and the family is staying in a cabin near the shore. These cabins are cheap in winter; nobody even bothers to ice fish around here. It is so cold. You are eight. Your brother is eleven and demands that you accompany him on a walk by the lakeside.

"We might see bears," he says, "but don't be scared." Your brother is eleven. He knows where the bears are.

Michigan winters are a Neverland to you. You remember The North as a fairy world, an icy magic wonder, far from the warmth of home. You realize, even then at eight years old, that this is slightly corny. You do not tell your brother how pretty you think everything is—the whiteness, the crystally twinkling of the sunlight on all the whiteness, the snow, the ice. It doesn't matter that you didn't tell him. He is going to die anyway.

You walk on the ice lake, walk and walk, until the shore and cabin are gone, until you reach huge ice lumps, frozen waves. They are huge, higher than both of your heads. You are not sure you believe these are waves. Your brother walks around them, looking. His thick black coat is trimmed with an orange cord that travels up his arms, around his hood. He looks perfectly warm.

"I wonder how that happened," he says. "It doesn't seem like that's what it is."

You still don't know if you really walked out that far on the lake. You still don't know, all these years after your brother has died, if you remember it correctly. You just remember the huge, white lumps, the clean ice, the stillness. Are you right? There is no way to know. No one else can remember it.

***

Your brother is going to die in two months. He is such a lazy bastard. He lies in bed, has stolen the whole morning, stolen your favorite quilt. Stolen it. You are leaving in a few minutes, going abroad for the first time in your life, on an airplane and everything. You won't see him again for at least another three months. You will never see him again. He is too goddamn lazy to get out from under your favorite quilt, the one with the white border, the one with all the triangles, and say goodbye. You are twenty.

"Come hug me," he says. "I love you."

You sigh and lie down next to him. He still smells the same as always, only spicier. He wears cologne now, and you breathe in traces of it. You have been glad to be in his home for a few days. You feel between things, lost. You are afraid to go someplace where you don't speak the language, but you are even more frightened of not going. His house has been a real thing, a few days of stability, but now you're leaving again. Your brother does not smell like he is going to die.

The bed, laid with your favorite quilt with the triangles, feels so warm. The lumps of his body—shoulders, knees, feet—swirl and swell under the quilt, rolling and arcing like the Blue Ridge outside the window. Your grandmother made that quilt, her mind wandering to the Cumberland Gap, her mind wandering, wandering for her lost children, wandering as she sewed each little piece. So you have kept it, that quilt. You wish you could stay, but the feeling passes quickly. You hug him for a moment and get up to leave. Your feet flop on the hardwood floor. He rotates and adjusts his head on the pillow as you turn back. He speaks softly as you leave, his voice muffled:

"Goodbye."

***

It is Christmas. It is another Christmas. And another. Another, another. You give unwelcome, unwanted gifts, the offerings of a younger sibling, badly painted, handmade, or broken, to your brother, who is going to die, and who pretends to like them, to know what you meant by them. The gifts get a little better every year. It seems to snow every year. You seem to always have been sleeping in the bed next to his on Christmas Eve. You seem to always have been unable to remember anything else about Christmas. You think of that often now.

***

Your brother is going to die in five and a half years. You have just finished watching *American Bandstand*. It is a Saturday afternoon, and you are trying to hide your huge, fat thighs by sitting in a beanbag, sitting with a pillow over your fat, huge, ugly thighs. You are fifteen. Your thighs are approximately eighteen inches in circumference.

Your brother, who is going to die, is playing records. You don't know what the music is, and you won't remember after he dies. His room is white. Painted, no longer his since he left home. The walls are freshly primed; the bedspread is white, the white, two-dollar pull-down blinds are pulled down. His hair is very, very dark brown. He stands in front of you, smiling, while you stay curled up in the beanbag on the floor. Your brother, who is going to die, smells like warm, clean linen. You can smell it from here, from the floor where your fat thighs are. Your brother, who will die, is dancing.

"Was it like this?" he says, trying to copy a move you have just seen on *Bandstand*. "Am I doing it right?"

You laugh. He holds out his hand and asks you to try it, too. You stand, and the two of you move easily, together, separately, together, swirling and grooving.

***

Your brother will be dead in one and a half years. It is Christmas. The whole family has come to visit your brother in the little town where his Big New Job is, his Big New House. The house sprawls and squats, a real bungalow, with wide porches and drystone walls in the yard outside, pillars, beadboard, a view of the Balsam Mountains. On the front porch there are so many wind chimes, left behind by the previous owner, that you cannot sleep at night.

You share a bed with your brother for three nights. It snows on Christmas Eve. You lie in bed and talk about a few things. You are both grown up, but you accuse each other of stealing the covers. You giggle. There are so many people in this house, so many spoons in the ramshackle kitchen downstairs, so many things. It is so cold outside. It snows; the wind blows. You laugh and fight.

You wish desperately, because he will be dead in a year and a half, that you had the courage to curl up into him like a nesting spoon. You can't remember the last time you did this, and you have no excuse to do so. You feel silly, so you do not ask. You look out the window and watch the white flakes swirling. The wind chimes jangle. You do not curl up against your brother, even though, for no reason, that is all you want to do. You wonder if he knows this.

You exchange good gifts this year. You can't remember what they were now.

***

You are two. You do not remember this, but you have been told. Your brother is going to school. You stand teetering at the screen door of your childhood home, screaming. The screen door has to be closed to keep you in, but the windows, big doors, everything is open. It is late summer, and so warm. Fans buzz around you, a low hum that drowns out the rest of the world. Your brother is leaving you, going to school. You are screaming his name. Or, at least, a version of his name. Your toddler mouth howls, calls his name, or whatever you think his name is. The tears streak your face; your diaper hangs lopsided from your waist. You do not remember this.

Your brother turns around and walks back to the house while you are screaming through the screen door. The school is only just across the road, but you do not know this. You only know he is leaving, and the white metal of the screen door is a barrier as you watch him go. You scream, even though he is coming back.

He comes back and brings you with him to the edge of the road. He holds your hand and walks with you.

"I'll be home soon," he tells you softly, "I won't be far away. See?" He points across to the school you do not recognize or see. His brown hair is downy and soft; his cheeks are full. He is only a little boy.

Someone, probably your mother, because she may be the one who told you this story, holds you back as your brother crosses the road. His legs are chubby, but he walks gracefully. He looks back and waves, then runs to the school on his chubby, graceful legs. You are tired from howling and crying, so you just watch him go, pouting. Your eyes are big, white saucers. He is leaving you.

You cry for the next five hours until he comes home.

You do not remember any of this.

***

He'll be dead soon. You are in Portugal, on that trip abroad you were so frightened of taking. You always seem to be leaving, trying to go somewhere. Your friends, or maybe your professors, have brought you to Fátima. After all this time, all the talk of miracles, Fátima is a huge disappointment. They are restoring the cathedral, so you can't go in. No tourists at this time of year, no restaurants, no stores open. The long, vast space in front of the cathedral is paved, pristine white concrete. There is no one here. You don't remember where your friends went or why you are alone in the huge, open space before the cathedral. You think you see a nun in the distance out of the corner of your eye, a black figure crossing the white pavement, but you're not sure.

The sky is low and thick with clouds. Your brother will be dead very, very soon.

You roam around the empty expanse of pavement, looking at fountains, statues, hedges, more statues. Our lady. Whatever. Everything is stone; everything has outstretched hands. The concrete around you is flat, white, empty of believers. The sky is grayish white and overcast. The pavement is an outstretched hand.

You sit under a hedge, on the very edge of the pavement, and write a postcard to your brother. All around you, total silence. You have no idea where everyone went.

***

Your brother is dead. It is hard to know anything else but this. Someone told you. An accident while hiking the old forest road. He was crushed, rent apart by some drunk trucker, some axle or unseen wheel. A lathe of evil twirling briefly the world, destroying its edges, for no reason. And now you are tired. Constantly. You drive your car for miles, for no reason, in the dark, screaming. For no reason. You cry for a whole year. You sleep for a whole year. You curl up under your favorite quilt, the one with the triangles, and you sleep for an entire year. You remember almost nothing about this year, except that you watched a lot of television. Your television was black and white. A white box, with silver and gray and white images playing constantly, incessantly. You sleep for a whole year.

***

Your brother is going to die in ten years. You know now, ten years after he is dead, that ten years before he died, you knew.

***

It is ten years until your brother will die. It is summer, and the two of you go for a walk. The cicadas trill loudly; it is early evening. The field behind your house is high with corn. Everything seems dry and hot. You walk and laugh; the two of you are funny. All kinds of things—books, stories, river birches—make you laugh. You are both so bright, such strong children under the hot sun. You run and fight and yell.

The country road is not paved, but you notice someone has covered the dirt track, put down a layer of long, thin slivers of tar. They are like black popsicle sticks, with big white flecks in them. You marvel at these; neither of you has ever seen them before. You pick up handfuls of them and throw them in the air, laughing.

When you get home from your walk, you look down and realize that bugs—chiggers, mosquitoes, something, you don't remember— have bitten you. Your legs. Your legs are covered in huge, red welts. They itch and hurt. They burn.

You look at your brother, but neither of you understands. Was it the popsicle sticks? The heat? Why didn't they bite him, too, whatever they were? You are in pain.

Your brother is thirteen, and he goes and gets cold water, rubbing alcohol, a towel, a soda. You don't remember where your parents were. Probably working. Your brother is thirteen—a young man.

"Hold still," he says. He kneels down and washes your legs and feet with cold water. You lean back on the old sofa. He puts alcohol on the welts. He sucks in air through his teeth in sympathy when you whimper from the sting of the alcohol. He gives you the soda.

You love him so much, and he takes care of you. You realize now, years and years after he has died, that he was dead long ago. He was dead when he did this, when he dressed your bug bites, because all the saints, at least the ones you can name, have always all been dead.

He is the only thing you notice or remember. You lean back on the sofa and look at the white and gold wallpaper while your drink fizzes next to you, and you realize you will still wonder someday, much later, what it was that bit you.

You realize, ten years before he is going to die, that you do not know if the frozen waves were real. You realize, ten years before, that you are going to want to curl up with him in the bungalow house on Christmas Eve. You realize, ten years, now, then, that he is a saint.

You realize this is a terrible thing.

You realize this is a terrible, terrible thing. To have a saint for a brother.

You realize that ten, fifteen, all the years after he dies it will be just as bad, just as hard.

You realize, somewhere, at some time, that none of this could ever have happened. There is no proof. There is no one who remembers these events but you. They become, then or now, like lost things. Like icicles, or faith.

You do not know where any of this starts or ends. You do not know, ten years before, or five months after, or in bed, or in the snow, or at the screen door, who your brother is or was. You look for him then, now, before, after, constantly.

You do not know when this started, and you do not know when or how it will ever end. Everything else feels sad and far away, all your life. Even now, years after. Even then.

You knew this would happen. You knew it all along.

SPARKLE

$\mathcal{J}$nside the cotton candy–pink ticket booth, Mavis—that's what her name tag said—shifted her ample, cardiganed breasts off the counter and looked out the customer window to see if there was anybody behind us.

"Now, it's not her usual thing," said Mavis when she'd decided we were alone. "But."

Behind me, James tensed. I figured it was going to be some kind of sales pitch for Splash Country, the water park next to Dollywood. James and I did not want to go to Splash Country. It was November, and it was raining. Mavis looked me square in the face.

"Bu-ut"—Mavis dropped her twang to an emphysemal whisper—"*Dolly* . . . is in the park today." She twitched her mouth and pursed it to the side, satisfied with herself, then placed her hands primly on the cotton candy windowsill.

"No shit," I said.

"Oh, yes, ma'am," said Mavis. Her hands went pat, pat, softly.

"James, did you hear that?" I looked at him and those eyebrows of his. James has these eyebrows that tell you everything. They raised up—a good sign.

"Oh, interesting," he said.

Heat tingled up the outside of my neck and into my cheeks. I stared into the little booth. Mavis winked. "I think I just peed a little," I said. Mavis thought that was funny.

"You go down there to the right," Mavis said, "and they's a little theater. Along about two thirty, she'll be in there."

My breath hitched. James closed in behind me until I could feel the warmth of him. Or maybe not the warmth. The ions of him? Electrons, crackling back and forth. That's how it is with certain people, now and then in life. You feel them even when they're not touching you.

"Is she . . ."—my turn to whisper—"Oh, Miss Mavis, will she sing?"

Mavis's face looked like a sack of dough, but I wanted to kiss it. Since I was thirteen, I have wanted to meet Dolly Parton, to exist for a minute in that cloud of glittery badassness. I don't even like country music. Just Dolly. All that *light*; she brings light into the world, or did into mine when I was a kid. In junior high, I'd sneak-watch VHS tapes of her. I'd plug my daddy's big stereo earphones into the back of the TV set so he wouldn't hear me. I spent most of my time making sure Daddy didn't wake up from his naps on the sofa; he'd punch the shit out of anybody who didn't let him sleep all afternoon. I'd patch into those earphones and whisper-sing Nine-to-five, Nine-to-five for hours, squatted on the living room rug. I never told my friends or watched those tapes with anybody.

Dolly's just about the only cheesy thing I can stand. I am not a cheesy person. Mavis was promising me something big here.

"No, honey," Mavis soothed. "It's an industry thing. A theme park conference? Bigwigs and such, park owners. Folks here from as far away as Knott's Berry Farm." She shifted back and rolled herself onto her little stool. I was glad the Dollywood people let Mavis have a stool in her ticket booth. She probably got tired standing all day. Mavis looked out the front window of her booth, the one facing into the park. "I don't reckon Dolly'll sing for those suited-up types. She's just gonna put in an appearance, do the welcome."

"Oh, I see," I said. My feet settled back into my shoes.

"But you never know. She knows people like for her to. And now"—Mavis leaned forward—"there'll still be music. Some good musicians in the park today, on all the corners."

James started to shimmy past me. We already had our tickets. He put his hand right below my bra strap as he made his way past. The warmth spread out from where his hand was, all over my back. After he eased by, he turned and gave me a come-on-already-let's-go look. So I went.

"All right, well, thank you so much for telling us," I said to Mavis.

"Sure thing. Two thirty, now. The orange doors." Mavis hopped off her stool and put her happy theme park face on for the next customer, even though there wasn't one. Most of the parking lots had been empty when we arrived. She called after us, "We're so glad to have you visiting with us here in Dollywood!"

I'm not obsessed with Dolly Parton or anything. I've only been to Dollywood four times in my whole life. I just wanted an excuse to be alone with James. He was only here for a few more days, and half of them were taken up with beer tours in Asheville and meetings in his old department. I couldn't get him alone at the house, either, because Pete kept muscling in. Also, Pete had been super touchy with me all week, all honey this and baby that, like all of a sudden we haven't been married for nine years. It made me itch.

We walked forward into the entrance gazebo. An elderly man with suspenders and an old-timey mustache took our tickets.

"Nice 'stash," James mumbled, one eyebrow raised.

Then we swooped out of the gazebo and into the park. All the colors and music stopped James in his tracks. James had never been to Dollywood. I paused and let him get accustomed. It's a lot to take in if it's your first time.

"Come on, Dorothy," I said. "Get your slippers on!"

It was early November, so there were no Christmas decorations up yet. The wind grayed everything over, and the mountains slumped brown and spindly above us, with no leaves left anywhere. We probably picked just about the dullest, drabbest day to go to such a place. But it's like Dolly made the park so it would be nice even in weather like that, because all the color she brings came right at us in a friendly way. The soft blue of the kiddie play area sat low at the edge of the view, and the pastels from the gospel music house windows eased us onto the main path toward the roller coasters. Nothing garish or harsh about it.

James got moving soon after the initial shock of the place. We walked to the right until we got to the candy stores. A wide, bright path led toward the county fair rides. Beyond that were the steam train, the bird sanctuary, roller coasters, old-timey shops, and on and on. From where we stood, the layers of the park loomed in blurry, then blurrier layers of neon and noise, one behind the other, getting indistinct and higher, just like the Blue Ridge does on a fine day.

"Whoa," James said, swaying toward a lavender storefront. "Do you smell that?"

I nodded. *Be breezy*, I thought. Don't spoil anything. This is the man you love.

Nobody knows I love James. Nobody. I can't breathe it out to anyone because all our friends work at the college and know Pete. Besides, it's just about the most embarrassing thing in the world, to need a man you can't have, aren't married to. But I still thought, *This is the man you love,* to myself down deep.

That's why we came to Dollywood. That's why I picked a day Pete had to teach, a day James wasn't giving any presentations, to suggest this trip. I pretended it was a whim that morning, something I'd just thought of. After Pete left for the lab, I sat at the breakfast table and laced this careful pattern of chatter with James to get him to come here with me. I know I just work in the bursar's office at the college, but I'm pretty smart when I want to be.

One other thing I know is, even though he doesn't love me, James thinks I'm the funniest person in the world. He always says that, and he always talked to me when I came to department parties, and sometimes took me out to lunch, just the two of us.

When he first started teaching at the college, James picked Pete as his research partner for an NSF grant he got. All about efficient light refraction on metallic particles, which Pete knew about. Pete did his master's at the college, and then he got hired on at the lab right before we met. On our first dates, Pete would talk about his work in a slow, plodful way that made me feel safe. Here was a man with purpose, someone you didn't have to be scared of waking. Pete let me be clumsy without picking on me, took me to Georgia to his parents' house, which always smelled like potpourri and clean money. I married him mostly because he asked.

James showed up a few years after, and he took to Pete right away. James says Pete missed his chance at a bona fide scientific career, and Pete knows more than anybody about what they do. But Pete isn't much for moving outward. He stayed plodful, stuck to the lab and his regularities. When I started to complain about the sameness in our life a few years back, Pete quit touching me. Or maybe I quit touching him. It doesn't matter now, after how long it's been.

Anyhow, James came, and a switch got thrown inside me. It didn't take any time at all before James decided he liked me as much as he did Pete. Like I said, I can be smart, and I'm pretty enough to get a man to buy me lunch now and then. There were even times when I thought James might love me back, just a little, because of how he'd look at me when he thought I wasn't noticing. Then he took a job down in the Piedmont at a fancier school, and now every time I see him it's like starting over from scratch.

But for the four years he was here, we saw each other a lot—

twice a week sometimes. We smoothed together so easy. James isn't from here, so he liked that I knew about the mountains. He'd ask me where to hike, which trees were blooming in the spring. He liked the stories I told about my family especially. His favorite was about the time my cousin Bigun climbed in the washer at our papaw's house when we were kids and got himself stuck.

We called him Bigun because he was a foot taller than anyone else we ever saw. I used to love playing with him because he treated me so gentle. Bigun used to tell me I was dainty. We'd play rock-paper-scissors, and Bigun always let me win, even though he was older than me and knew better. He'd wait for me to count three and flatten my fingers; then he'd make a meaty fist at the last second and smile out of every part of his face. It took both my hands spread out wide to paper over Bigun's rock.

James was eating a muffin at the hippie coffee shop by the campus library when I told him the yarn about Bigun getting stuck in the washer. He laughed so hard he choked on a muffin chunk. There were little muffin bits on my clothes when I walked out and headed back to my desk, but I didn't mind. I got to pat James on the back and hold his shoulder and ask close if he was all right, even though I knew he was fine.

Three weeks before James came back for this visit, I found an old Dollywood souvenir mug at the Methodist thrift store. I bought it for a quarter. This morning after Pete left, I gave James that mug when he said he wanted more coffee. I asked him about his plans, even though I knew them. I'd looked up his schedule in the department secretary's office. I brought him his coffee and spun chatter for a few minutes. I kept him laughing, dazzled, then finally struck, *Oh, hey, . . . you know what we should do?* and pointed at the mug, with Dolly's face on it and a big chip on her boob. Breezy.

I'd been wanting to bring him here ever since I found out he was coming for a whole week this time and staying at our house. Finding that mug was proof, a sign. I wanted to go to the brightest

place I could think of and stare at James for as long as I could before he was gone again.

James is normal handsome, nothing special. He's kind of bald,
and he has this goofy left eye that doesn't sit on his face the same
way as his other one. But I love him; have since the first day I saw
him. For all my sins, I love a hairless, lop-eyed chemist so bad it
makes my whole body hurt when I so much as sit next to him. It
hurts way inside, like cramps or sickness.

It hasn't been a problem lately, because James hasn't been here.
He visits for this one silver project he still works on, but that's twice
a year at most. I think about him though, just as much as I did for
the four years he was here. I keep waiting for that storm of feeling
to go away or settle in me somewhere far down, but it hasn't. I figure it won't ever. Once I get an idea I tend to hang on to it pretty
tight.

Maybe I am a cheesy person after all. I don't know. But James
said yes when I offered to bring him to Dollywood, and he laughed
when he said it, and he couldn't think of a better way to spend his
free day, and he'd be ready by ten, and we could go. So it worked,
my spinning and scheming. That's all I cared about.

"Caramel," James said. His eyes were closed, his body facing
the candy storefront. "We could get caramel apples. Do they have
those?"

"We haven't even seen anything yet," I said. I pulled him down
the path. I tried to sound chummy, so I had an excuse to lean into
him. I couldn't smell any caramel. I could only smell the cedar-
wood tang of the soap he uses. I made sure I bought some before
he came and put it in the spare bathroom. "Don't go soft on me so
soon. There's hoot owls and roller coasters and all kinds up there.
And we're going to Dolly's house—you have to see it. Candy's for
later."

The sky looked like dirty quilt batting, and we walked past the
sausage and peppers stand, the bluegrass gazebo, and a bunch of

other stuff, waiting for a drop of sunlight. Mavis was right; some of
the music was pretty good.

We got to the center of the park, and I showed James to Dolly's
house, the one she grew up in. It's right where Dolly wants it, beside
a bunch of lit-up signs for attractions and souvenir shops, with
about five different places to eat circled around it. The cabin is on
an island in the middle of all that bustle, just below the railroad
bridge at the main intersection, so nobody forgets where Dolly
came from.

James stepped up on the walkway with just his toe tips and read
the sign carefully while I stood behind him. Then he said, "Are we
allowed in?" He turned to me, and his face was like a boy's. I don't
imagine very many people ever get to see his face like that.

I nodded and pointed to the sign, and we went inside. The tour
only takes a minute, because Dolly grew up in a three-room house.
They put most of the historical stuff, like her gowns and her coat
of many colors, in her personal museum farther down in the park.
Here in the cabin, glass barriers keep everyone out to preserve the
place exactly as it was when she was a little girl. A sack of flour still
sits by the stove, and the wallpaper is nothing but old newspapers.

All the noise of the park, the rides, the railroad, all of it drains
away inside Dolly's cabin. The only thing we could hear was the
boats swirling through the Smoky Mountain River Rampage down
the hill. Each boat goes around a track and gets to a point where
the fake rocks squirt river water all over the passengers. The whole
thing works on a timer, I guess, because James and I walked along
so softly inside the old place, and he whispered all his comments
and questions to me, and everything hushed into respectful silence,
except for about every twenty seconds or so, when we'd hear *thock-
thock-shwhoosh*.

We finished the cabin tour and came out by the railroad bridge,
and James said, "Well, that was incongruently tasteful." He knitted
up his forehead and walked up toward the blacksmith shops. "She's

really something, isn't she? Quite a beginning." He turned back to the cabin and regarded it from a higher vantage point.

Then he peered at me. His face wasn't boyish now; he looked detached, like he was researching something. He lifted his head and jutted his chin back down the hill toward Dolly's cabin. "Did you grow up in a place like that?"

Well, I mean please. My face went hot, and my stomach whomped fiercely. I couldn't decide if I was heartbroken or pissed. I tried to slow my breathing so my gut wouldn't hurt.

"No, Professor," I said. I crossed my arms and looked up the hill, away from him, toward the sunlight diffused behind all that dirty cotton batting. I was looking for the blue wings of the eagle coaster way up top. "I had plumbing and everything."

"Oh. Oh, right. I'm sorry, Beth."

"Heck, I even read a few books when I was a kid, when I wasn't losing teeth." I turned back to him and raised my chin. "Even managed to gra-jee-ate college."

"Of course. I didn't mean . . ."

"You want lunch?" I started walking. "Let's get some peppers and sausage."

"Beth, I'm sorry."

"Sure, fine. Just . . . you know. I'm not a country-fried fool or anything."

"I know that. I know it."

The whitewater boats *thock-shwooshed* again, far down the hill.

"It's just—I think you're like her," James said. He sounded far away. "Like Dolly."

"Quit looking at my tits, Doc."

"No, really." I knew he was trying to smile, but I wouldn't look at him. I followed a crack in the blacktop under my foot. It went on forever.

"I intended it as a compliment," he said. "Of course, you dress much more simply." He seized on a word and blurted, "More re-fined."

Then he rubbed his head, put his hands in his pockets, and shrugged roughly. He rocked on his feet and leaned against the sign for Aunt Granny's Restaurant. I remembered then not everyone thinks James is as beautiful as I do. Scientists move like awkward birds, and he does have that thing with his left eyeball, after all. So I let go of the insult. At least he'd tried to make up for it by calling me refined.

"How long till two thirty?" I asked.

James bent deeply to pull his hand from his pocket and frowned at his watch. "We've got about an hour." He turned and squinted at the eagle coaster on the hill.

For the record, the eagle coaster at Dollywood kicks ass. It looks like a giant bird, and the seats don't have a floor. People swing their legs free and scream their faces off on that thing. I've never ridden on it because every time I've been to Dollywood that coaster is shut down for bees. Apparently there are bee colonies up on top of the hill, and Dolly doesn't want to mess with them or move them. So instead, if the bees are lively in summertime, they put up a special sign with honey pots and smiling bumblebees on it, and no one can ride the eagle coaster until they settle down into their hives.

It was late autumn now, with all the sun and leaves over, so no bees. The eagle was running—a giant raptor swaying above us, all blue and shiny, even under the dark, low clouds.

James watched the blue wings of the coaster for a second and said, "I don't really do stuff like that anymore. It twinges my back."

I watched a few little kids run screaming up the hill toward the bird and clenched my jaw. My mother never used to bother telling me to have babies because she knows I don't want any. Kids are supposed to make you tender, but I never feel any closeness inside me when I see one. Anytime I see children, they seem far away.

But lately when she visits, Mama says it—get pregnant already.

Then she shakes her head at me and says I'm gloomy. She says our house is too quiet. It took her years to figure out Pete doesn't hit me, because she just figures that's what everybody lives with. She thinks the way I grew up is normal.

My mother. She sees I'm missing something, but she doesn't know what it is.

It took me a second to let go of the idea of finally riding the eagle coaster. I breathed out slow and said, "Well, you want lunch then?" I put a little singsong in my voice to tease him, "Yo-u can have can-dy af-ter . . ."

He smiled, but only from one side of his face, then bowed and swooped his hand toward the food stalls like a butler in some old movie. "Sausage and peppers, it is, madame."

We found a picnic area with seats made out of old barrels sawed in half and smooshed butt side up into the concrete. James didn't talk much over lunch, so I told him another story about Bigun to entertain him. This story was more recent, after Bigun grew up, a year or so before I met James. I told about Bigun getting drunk and shooting his rifle into the Dairy Queen sign when they forgot to put the peanuts on his sundae. I didn't tell James about Bigun crashing his pickup a few days later, or how he lingered in the ICU, broken and swollen like an angry tick, for six weeks before he finally passed. I didn't say how I spread out my textbooks on the plastic sofa outside his room and studied for all my semester exams, peeking in every now and then to see if Bigun's fingers would twitch hello for me. I didn't want to talk about sad things before we saw Dolly. Bigun's real name was Charles, so I told him that instead.

A little after two we wound our way to the theater. We went to the orange doors just like Mavis said, and it turned out Mavis is kind of a blabbermouth because there must have been two hundred people already in line. A lot of them were suited-up types, with name tags from a bunch of different theme parks pinned to their lapels. But about half the crowd was regular people like us.

I wondered where they'd all been hiding up to now; the park had been empty all afternoon.

"Betrayed," James said, shaking his head. "I assumed our ticket lady was keeping this between friends."

"It'll be fine. We'll get a seat," I replied. "Doesn't matter as long as we get to see her."

James nodded, and we got in line. We filed in through the big orange doors, and we found seats way at the back of the main floor, off to the far left. The seats were dark blue and thick cushioned. Everything on the stage was blue, too. Blue curtains and a big TV screen with nothing on it except the royal emptiness you get on channels you haven't paid for. James said he figured we'd have to sit through some conference talk before we got to see Dolly, and he asked if I was up for it. I said yes, I'd sat through my share of boring presentations with Pete. Turned out we didn't have to wait long at all.

A round, standard-issue Yankee in a navy suit came up onstage to give a speech about the national federation of theme park executives, or whatever it was called, and how pleased they were to be there, and what the schedule for today's keynote event would be. He was just getting to the part where he asked everyone to check their conference schedule booklet when a gleeful surge rumbled over from the right side of the house. I looked across the stage, and there she was.

Dolly Parton, right there in front of me.

They say celebrities look smaller in person, and it's a disappointment because you expect them to be taller or more imposing. When Dolly walked out, my mouth dropped open, and I shot out of my seat. As I watched her, I thought two things at the same time: she was the littlest, tiniest thing I'd ever seen, and she wasn't a disappointment at all. All the typical stuff you think of when you think of Dolly Parton—shine and light and makeup and hair and boobs—all of it was perfect. She looked so totally and exactly like I wanted her to, I almost didn't believe it was her. Her being so little made me think she was a doll, a fancy toy for rich kids. Then I forgot about her smallness and held my hands together tight and watched her walk toward the guy in the suit. He had dropped his conference booklet and was beaming silently.

I don't care who you are. Everybody in that room was overcome. James shot to his feet right along with me, and he was clapping and watching her, then turning to me and laughing, back and forth. Dolly looked so beautiful, and she was smiling and waving to everyone. She stood there for just the right, dignified amount of time, not too long, and let the crowd applaud her. A sound guy in a black T-shirt ran out and handed her a microphone.

"Well, hey, everybody!" Dolly Parton giggled at us.

We all waved and applauded some more, and she waved back. James crossed his arms and put one elbow on his hand so he could raise the opposite hand to his chin and rest it there. Every last one of us, even the suits who were acting businesslike while we were in line, all of us were transfixed.

Dolly must have known they'd have all blue up there, because she had chosen a gold outfit that stood out against the blue backdrop and popped off the stage. She had on a slinky gold satin dress, sleeveless. It glistened softly down to her knees. That dress would have been a classy number by itself, but it's Dolly, so over the dress she wore a jacket I won't ever forget. The jacket looked like the finest lace, only it was bright gold and twinkly everywhere. It had to have been handmade, and it didn't look cheap. She stood in front of the big blue TV screen, and between that and the spotlight hitting her, the gold jacket reflected and refracted back and forth to build a fine, warm halo around her. I know that sounds crazy, and I'm not going to say she looked like an angel on top of a Christmas tree, but I'll bet that's what a bunch of us were thinking. James studies light-refracting particles, so he probably knew exactly what was making Dolly shine.

She didn't stay for long. Mavis was right; she had only come to welcome the conference attendees. Apparently that conference is a big deal in theme park circles. Dolly said she had come out today to tell all the theme park executives how glad she was they had chosen Dollywood to host their big meeting. She talked about the history of the park, how it used to be called Silver Dollar City before she bought it and fixed it up.

Some woman behind me said, "That's right, you remember, Dan? She saved the place. I used to come here and ride that ol' run-down silver mine coaster." I nudged James to see if he'd heard.

Then Dolly made one of her usual jokes about her boobs, and she told the suits to be sure and tell her what they thought of her little ol' theme park, because she and her staff had worked hard to make it a great place for folks to come with their families. Then she thanked us again and thanked the boring guy in the navy suit for letting her steal some of his time. She handed him the microphone and walked off waving and blowing kisses.

The audience clapped and hollered, but Dolly didn't come back out to sing. We settled down slowly, but the whole theater tingled for a long time after. Whatever electrons James shoots into me when he's nearby, Dolly's got a billion more of them, because everyone in there felt warm and happy. Mr. Blue Suit never stopped beaming while he said three times Dolly was "marvelous." Then he said his colleagues should wait a minute for park visitors to file out of the theater, and then the conference would proceed on schedule.

We were all in such a good mood nobody minded bustling and squishing past each other in the narrow aisles. As I shimmied toward the orange exit, I checked everyone's faces. All the suits looked tickled and loose. James and I said excuse me and I'm sorry a hundred times, and we got patted on the shoulder if we accidentally stepped on a foot or a briefcase. Dolly eases people.

When we got outside, I could tell James was impressed. I asked him, "Well, was that the highlight of your week?" He put his hands on his hips and smiled with all his teeth; then he shrugged big. He didn't have to say anything. My whole body shook, but I kept my own thoughts inside so I wouldn't spoil his.

"You want to get that caramel apple now?" I asked. "The shop's over there."

James put one hand on his belly, and I noticed his fleece jacket was the same color as our theater seats. His face darkened. "I probably shouldn't. I just ate that sausage. Besides," he said, "who needs candy when you've got Dolly Parton?"

I laughed. "Nothing sweeter, right?"

"Yes, she really does have something. I was impressed. Dazzled, even." James patted his stomach, then arced his hand to indicate the park, the rides, Dolly, the wide, bright paths, Mavis in the ticket booth, everything. "All that glitters," he murmured.

We strolled through the candy shops but didn't buy anything. James took one look at the caramel apples and said they were as big as a baby's head. I pretended to look at cookbooks. Mostly I peeped at James between the bookshelves, especially when he walked through the lollipop section. Some of those lollipops span a foot across, and they stack up in rows along the walls. Against the swirling candy behind him, the subtlety of his dark-blue jacket and his brown hair popped. He stood out the same way golden Dolly had popped on that blue stage, but it was like James was doing it in reverse, a negative of an old color photograph.

There's not much left to Dollywood once you get past the candy stores. We'd left all the rides and kids' stuff behind us. James wasn't interested. It was pretty much just the gift shop left. You can't leave Dollywood unless you go through the gift shop; it's the only exit.

I figured James would buy something since he hadn't ridden any of the rides. A little part of me hoped he'd buy *me* something, to thank me for bringing him, signify the day, so I remarked on a few items. I made sure not to be girly about it, but he didn't pick up or touch anything. I even found a mug exactly like the chipped one

I bought at the Methodist thrift store. I showed him. He nodded and mm-hmmed in a friendly way that meant no.

"You don't want a souvenir?" I finally asked. "It's the same as my mug from this morning, but without the crack on her tit."

James tilted his head. "I've got a bunch of luggage I need to take home."

"So, but, you had fun, right? Isn't this place a kick?"

"Yes, I'll admit I did have fun, actually." He smiled again and turned away slightly. Then he mumbled, "To be honest, I was expecting Araby."

I rolled my eyes. What a thing to say. James squinted and leaned toward me.

"Araby," he said again slowly. "That's, uh . . . It's a story."

"Yeah." I plonked the Dolly mug back on the table and glared at a row of shot glasses to my right. "There's a copy of *Dubliners* on the shelf in the spare room. You can borrow it later."

"Oh, right. Sure. Sorry, I just assumed you wouldn't . . ."

"We should head back," I said. "It'll take us at least an hour. More if it starts to rain."

Those shot glasses. They all looked so clear and clean. The fluorescent bulbs above us shone straight down to the bottom of each one and made a pool of light that splashed up through their silver lettering.

"Yes, you're right," said James. "Hey, did you want to get anything for yourself? Those hats are sort of neat." He pointed to a high shelf lined with baseball caps covered in glittery butterflies. Butterflies are Dolly's mascot.

"I don't wear hats." I leaned into my hip. "We can catch a trolley back to the car."

As I moved to go, I felt my fingers reach out to the shot glasses on our way past. I grabbed one and stuffed it in my pocket in one blunt, smooth swipe. There.

We walked past the stuffed animals and toys to the door, back out into the cold late afternoon. To the right, a series of ropes wound along a plain concrete tunnel. The end of each rope marked where visitors could wait for a lift. We moseyed along the tunnel, me with my hands shoved in the back pockets of my jeans, shoulders wide, James hunched over thinking to himself about something that was probably far away from here. I wondered whether he even noticed the mountains glowing lavender at their edges in the late afternoon gloom.

When we got to the front of the line, he said, "Well, I guess we can die happy, now that we've seen Dolly Parton in all her glory."

I snorted. "Hardly."

I don't know if it was his question about living in a shack, or not getting to ride the eagle coaster, or skipping the gift shop, or what, but all of a sudden I felt hard toward James. He didn't know. It wasn't his fault, but I hated him then, and I wanted the trolley to come soon, fast.

Because I have all this love. I feel it in me and around me like those electric sparks that come out of magicians' hands in old movies. The sparks crackle and swell all the time, but he doesn't see it spilling out of me.

I don't understand that. Not at all.

"Oh?" James smiled back. He didn't know. "So, what then, Miss Tennessee? What do you need to die happy?"

I sighed. I could see the trolley coming, a chain of long white golf carts strung together. They were hitched up loose, so the whole thing writhed like a huge maggot as it drove up. It turned from the entrance, from the ticket booths where we met Mavis, and came toward us.

"Take me to a hotel tonight," I said.

I blinked hard. His face tilted; his eyebrows in three different positions each. I crossed my arms and stepped out to meet the trolley. It beeped and tooted all kinds of happy noises that echoed off the concrete and hurt my ears. "You do that," I said. "You take me away for a night, just once, and I'll go to my grave."

I could feel the rattle in my voice coming, the quiver that rises when you're about to cry, so I bit down and focused on the maggot stopping in front of us. A sharp laugh shot out of me.

"But that's not going to happen, right? You're not going to fuck some redneck. So." I shrugged. "Guess I can't die."

I spat the last few words and climbed into an empty trolley seat.

"Goooood evening, folks!" the trolley driver chirped into the PA system. "We'll be on our way just as soon as everyone gets on safely."

Almost no one was waiting with us, but the trolley idled for a few minutes in case more people came looking for a ride. I don't know how long it took before James finally sat down next to me. I don't know if he stared at me, or laughed, or looked back at the eagle coaster and felt bad inside. I kept my eyes on the white floor of the maggot and waited to get hurt.

I sensed his electron warmth before too long. He scooted up close. The glinty shot glass I'd stolen had worked its way into the crevice between my hip and crotch. It sat there like a thick bullet.

"Elizabeth."

"Just fuck off for a minute, James."

"Awwwwwrighty folks," the trolley driver chirped again. "We are taking off, and we'll have you to your ve-hickles in no time. Please make sure your packages are secure, and hold on to your little ones."

"Is it . . ." James nodded at a perky trolley attendant who was waving frantic goodbyes to everyone on the maggot. "Have you always felt like this?"

"Yep."

We drove to Lot A and stopped. We were parked in Lot C.

"I'm shocked," he finally said. His eyes widened and he turned toward me. "I mean, I'm flattered, but I'm just—shocked." He touched his chest.

"How?"

"What?"

"How is that possible? How can you be shocked?"

"Well, I . . . Beth, you're married."

Pete. Fucking Pete. As if Pete counts as being married. Pete was an obstacle. He blocked everything. Pete could block the sun.

"You seriously don't notice it? This?" I pointed back and forth between us until James's eyes softened. "You never think about it."

"Yes, sure. I've thought about it. Of course I have."

"Lot B, folks. This is Lot B," the driver announced.

"So what then? You don't think it would work? You don't even want a fling or anything? Jesus, why not get a little action when you're in town, at least?" I was keeping it breezy, even now.

James stared straight ahead for a full minute, until I figured he hadn't heard, or he'd never answer me. The trolley was approaching our lot when he spoke again.

"If we were both single, if I still lived here, sure, maybe. But Beth. That's not the way things are. And Pete . . . you know." He shook his head and grunted with a harsh edge I'd never heard before. The maggot came to a stop. "Pete's a pretty good friend of mine."

"So OK then, folks!" the driver shouted. "This is Lot C. Please step out on the right, and thank y'all for visiting us here in Dolly-wood! We hope you had a great time today. Come see us again." The trolley radio squawked and fired up again. "Passengers going into the park, please step in on the left. Please secure your belong-ings and hang on to your little ones."

There were no passengers going into the park, no little ones. James and I stepped out on the right, I think. I wasn't paying atten-tion, and I couldn't see in front of me. My eyes were welled up and everything looked like frosted bathroom glass. I didn't cry, though.

It didn't take long to walk to the car. The lot was empty now.

I held out my car keys to James and tried to keep my voice light. "You want to drive me home?"

He reached, curled his hand over the keys, and kept his arm held out to me for a long second. I looked at his fingers. They looked like mine, but stronger, more manly. I wanted to bend down and rest my cheek on them, soft like a newborn, for as long as I could, long enough to memorize his knuckles, the grooves at the base of his palm, how they felt against my skin. But I knew how girlish and strange it would seem, me bent double over somebody's fist in a cold, empty parking lot, and for no reason. It wouldn't mean anything to do it.

So instead I said, "We could take the back route, through the national park, instead of the interstate. It's just as quick."

It wasn't just as quick, but I didn't want to deal with all the traffic and neon signs in Gatlinburg or go too fast. The sky had been woolen all afternoon, and soon the daylight would be gone.

"Sure, Beth," he said, more breath than words. And I figured that was nice of him. He would take the wheel and leave me be all the way home.

As we pulled out, I thought about Dolly's gold jacket, how it floated on her like lacy sparkle wings, all the way down, almost to the floor. I couldn't fit one arm into a jacket like that without ripping it. Then I thought about the silver particles floating in tubes in the lab James and Pete used to share, the glitter soup they'd make for their experiments. I liked when they made it, but I was never allowed to get too close because Pete said the particles were growing and forming, swapping and stealing atoms from each other, and even a fingerprint on the beaker could upset the balance.

All the delicate things in the world that shine like that. I looked back toward Dollywood, and I thought about all of them. They shine on their own, and they break if I ever try to get them in my hands.

Acknowledgments

This book was made possible by my husband, Joel; my family; my agent, Julia Kenny; and Caroline Zancan, Kerry Cullen, and everyone at Holt.

Deepest gratitude to the friends, mentors, and editors who helped these stories along: Edward Carey, Elizabeth McCracken, Naomi Shihab Nye, Lara Prescott, Rachel Heng, Maria Reva, Sindya Bhanoo, Kate Kelly, Olga Vilkotskaya, Nouri Zarrough, Marla Akin, Jim Magnuson, Terry Kennedy, Belle Boggs, Wilton Barnhardt, Margaret Bauer, Liza Weiland, Anna Lena Phillips Bell, Beth Staples, Brandon Taylor, Robert Gipe, David Joy, Silas House, Jason Howard, Charles Dodd White, Denton Loving, Elizabeth Glass, Mark Powell, Wesley Browne, Sarah Ivens Moffett, Mimi Fenton, Darnell Arnoult, Steve Scafidi, Tracie Matysik, Wiley Cash, Robyn Shaw Cnockaert, and the TSWT writers group. Special thanks to everyone in my beloved Michener cohort and my Hindman family.

The following institutions/entities generously supported my work: the Appalachian Writers Workshop at Hindman, the Michener Center for Writers, Hedgebrook, the Vermont Studio Center, the Mountain Heritage Literary Festival, the University of

Texas at Austin, Wildacres Retreat, A-BTech Community College, Western North Carolina Arts Council, North Carolina Writers Network, North Carolina State University, the Adirondack Center for Writing, and the Stadler Center for Poetry and Literary Arts.

About the Author

Leah Hampton is a graduate of the Michener Center for Writers. The winner of the University of Texas at Austin's Keene Prize for Literature, she is also the recipient of North Carolina's James Hurst and Doris Betts prizes for fiction. Her work has appeared in *storySouth*, *Electric Literature*, *McSweeney's Internet Tendency*, *Appalachian Heritage*, *North Carolina Literary Review*, the *Los Angeles Times*, *Ecotone*, and elsewhere. A former college instructor, Hampton lives in and writes about the Blue Ridge Mountains.